NO STRINGS ATTACHED

HARPER BLISS

Also by Harper Bliss

The Road to You
Far from the World We Know
Seasons of Love
Release the Stars
Once in a Lifetime
At the Water's Edge
French Kissing: Season Three
French Kissing: Season Two
French Kissing: Season One
High Rise (The Complete Collection)

Copyright © 2016 Harper Bliss
Cover picture © Depositphotos / belchonock
Cover design by Caroline Manchoulas
Published by Ladylit Publishing – a division of Q.P.S. Projects Limited -
Hong Kong

ISBN-13 978-988-14909-8-8

For everyone who is in the closet.
I hope you find a good way out.

CHAPTER ONE

"To one year of freedom." Amber held up her cup of green tea.

Micky stared into her latte and shook her head. "Let's not toast to that." She looked up and found Amber's eyes. "Freedom's overrated."

Amber cocked her head. "What's wrong with you today? This is not the effect my yoga class is supposed to have." She kept holding up her mug.

Micky averted her glance. Amber was always beaming with positive energy and obvious physical and mental health. Some days, it was just too much. "I'm not saying I'm not happy that my divorce became official exactly one year ago, but I don't have that much to show for it. This yoga session is the highlight of my week. My children don't need me anymore, which they keep reminding me of at every turn. I had foolishly believed my life would become better after leaving Darren, but it doesn't feel that way."

"You're still finding your feet. And Olivia and Christopher do still need their mother very much. They're still getting used to the situation as well. Think long-term, Micky."

"Well, I definitely don't want to get back with Darren, I just… feel so empty, so meaningless. My days are filled with literally doing nothing."

"They're filled with the exact same activities as before the divorce. It's just your perspective that's different," Amber said.

Amber was a good friend to have, but her spiritual

mumbo jumbo did irritate Micky at times like these. Micky could also do with a glass of New Zealand sauvignon blanc much more than this latte.

Micky shrugged as Kristin, The Pink Bean's owner, headed in their direction.

"Hello, ladies," she said. "I hope you had a good class."

Micky let Amber reply to that question. Amber explained how she'd had her students stay in pigeon pose for longer than usual and asked Kristin when she was going to join again.

"As soon as I find a new employee." She thrust a sheet of paper in Micky's direction. "Are your children old enough to have an after-school job?"

"*My* children?" Micky bristled. "Actually work for pocket money?" She feigned an exaggerated laugh, then clasped a hand to her chest. "It's my own fault. I spoiled them too much."

"How about you, Micky?" Amber's voice rose.

"Me what?" Micky stared at the text on the piece of paper. *Barista wanted. Being upbeat is much more important than being experienced.*

"You're looking for something to do with your time. Why don't you apply?" Amber looked at Kristin, possibly for words of encouragement, but Kristin had a business to run so why would she hire a washed-up divorcée like Micky? And why would Micky take a job in the first place?

"It could be fun," Kristin weighed in. "You come in here every day, anyway. I'll show you the ropes."

"Me?" Micky leaned back. "Work at The Pink Bean?" The idea sounded ludicrous to her. "I don't know the first thing about making complicated cups of coffee like this."

"You're an expert at drinking them, though," Amber offered.

"Think about it." Kristin shot Micky an encouraging smile, then walked off and pinned the sheet of paper on the notice board by the door.

"Why did you say that in front of her?" Micky gave Amber a wry look.

"You know me, Michaela, I'm always only trying to help."

It was infuriating, but true. "Can you imagine me serving coffee at The Pink Bean?"

"Why not? You were just telling me about how empty you feel inside. You basically said you're bored. Working here for a few hours a day can change that. You'd meet new people. You wouldn't be alone. And you can take my evening classes. They're a bit fuller, but I'll still pay special attention to you." Amber drew her lips into that wide smile of hers. A ginger curl had escaped from her ponytail and danced along her temple as she nodded.

"But"—and Micky was embarrassed to admit this—"I haven't worked a day in my whole life."

"What are you talking about?" Amber's voice rose again. For a yoga teacher, she really had problems keeping her voice level in social situations. "You raised two children. You made a home for them and for your ex-husband. It's not because you don't get paid for it that it isn't a job—and a tough one at that."

"If you put it that way." Was Micky actually starting to consider this crazy idea? What did she really have to lose apart from a few hours of her time, which she didn't do anything useful with, anyway. "But I've certainly never had a boss before."

"You live with two teenagers. No boss can be worse than that. Besides, Kristin is a pussycat." Amber let her gaze slide to the counter where Kristin was chatting to a customer. "Remember that time I hit on her because she was always alone in here and I read it all wrong and I assumed she was single?"

Micky nodded. "How could I forget when you remind me every few months?"

"She let me down so gently. It was the easiest rejection

I ever experienced. She even offered me a free cup of tea, which I didn't accept, of course."

Micky had heard the story of Amber's failed crush on Kristin many a time since The Pink Bean had opened two years ago. Since then, they'd met Kristin's wife Sheryl, a professor at the University of Sydney, and Amber had successfully gotten over her crush.

"What will my kids think of their mother working at a coffee shop called The Pink Bean?" No matter what she did, Micky's hormonal teenagers would disapprove noisily for an instant, then retreat back into the silence they wrapped themselves in with their oversized headphones on their heads and their blinking screens in front of their eyes.

"They won't mind, and it doesn't matter." Amber fixed her gaze on Micky's, as though wanting to say something with her intense stare.

"What?" Micky asked.

"You've let it slip that you might be open to… exploring more. This is a great place to start."

Micky's eyes grew wide. "What on earth—"

"Don't play innocent with me now. I'm your best friend. Have been for a very long time. I've seen your gaze wander. Besides, you've told me in no uncertain terms."

Micky felt herself flush. This didn't stop Amber from pushing further.

"On a day like today especially, on the first anniversary of your divorce, I think you should take action. Not just symbolic action. Real action. Make a change. Take a step forward."

At least Amber was letting go of the innuendo. "I'll sleep on it, I promise."

Amber nodded, then slanted her torso over the small table. "I know it wasn't the actual reason for the divorce, because there's never only one reason, but I know you're curious. It's time to put yourself out there."

Only Amber could say something like that and have the

most endearing, non-smug look on her face as she leaned back.

"When will *you* put yourself out there again?" Micky countered.

"I have," Amber was quick to say, then scrunched her lips together. "You know I have, I just haven't met the right woman yet."

"Maybe you're frequenting the wrong places and hanging out with the wrong kind of people." Micky was still a little unsettled by what Amber had just implied.

"You mean The Pink Bean and you?" Amber narrowed her eyes. "Never."

Micky looked around the cozy coffeehouse just round the corner from her new home—from her new life. She'd been living in the Darlinghurst area for only a few months, and had chosen this quickly gentrifying neighborhood at Amber's insistence. Amber claimed Micky couldn't hide herself away in the suburbs of Mosman anymore, not even if it meant that Olivia and Christopher would have much smaller bedrooms to sulk in.

Kristin gave her a quick wave from behind the counter. Micky tried to imagine herself behind it.

Should she take the leap?

CHAPTER TWO

When she'd gone hunting for a new pad, Micky had fallen in love with the second house the real estate agent had shown her. Her children, not so much. The biggest trade-off when they had swapped Mosman for Darlinghurst had, in the end, not been the size of the bedrooms but the fact the new house only had one bathroom they all had to share. On school days, Micky had no problem letting Olivia and Christopher take their showers first, the latter never spending more than five minutes in there anyway, while she made them breakfast and attempted—mostly in vain—to get them to eat it.

"I'll have an apple on the bus" was Olivia's standard reply, while Christopher would eat one forkful of the scrambled eggs she'd made, mumbling, "Mmm, good, Mom," just to placate her, after which he probably wolfed down a Snickers bar. Micky found the wrappers everywhere.

Today, though, Micky needed to be at The Pink Bean at seven thirty—"Just to observe on your first morning shift," Kristin had assured her—and she was impatiently waiting for Olivia to exit the bathroom. This reinforced the thought that this whole thing was an awful idea in the first place. She was forty-four years old. She'd been married to Darren Steele for a whopping eighteen of those—she'd given him her prime. What was she doing starting work at a coffee shop where, at least once a week, an LGBT activity took place?

Micky remembered the double-take she had done when Amber had first brought her there just after it opened.

"Must it really be so blatantly obvious?" she had asked,

not caring how that made her come across. Her marriage had been in the final stage of its existence and what if someone she knew ran into her at a coffeehouse called The Pink Bean. Why couldn't it just be called The Bean? And now she was going to work there—or at least attempt to. What did that say about her?

Her kids, who had become regulars at The Pink Bean as well, often going in after school for a muffin or an iced tea, didn't seem to be disturbed by the Pink aspect of The Bean when she told them about her plans. They'd mostly scoffed and said, "You, Mom? Serve people coffee? Why?"

Micky had explained that she needed something to do with her time, now that they obviously didn't need her that much anymore.

"But why do that?" Olivia had asked. "Can't you volunteer at a soup kitchen or something, like other moms?"

Micky had postponed and postponed her decision to leave Darren. She'd wanted to stay until both her children were at university, but Olivia was only twelve at the time and the six years it would take for her to graduate high school seemed like a lifetime.

Micky had not been able to provide Olivia with a coherent answer to her question. Not even *she* knew why she wanted to work at The Pink Bean—she didn't even know *if* she wanted to work there. It was just a leap, like Amber had said. Trying something new.

Christopher, who was a sweet boy at heart, but suffered deeply from the mood swings that come with puberty, hadn't been very talkative and had just grumbled something Micky didn't understand.

Micky knocked on the bathroom door. "Hurry up, Liv," she shouted, while nerves coursed through her body.

The bathroom door flew open, and Olivia stormed out. "Is it going to be like this every morning now?"

Tonight at dinner, Micky would suggest a proper morning bathroom schedule. She shouldn't have tried to wing it like this. "We'll work it out, sweetie." She resisted the urge to kiss her daughter on the top of the head—Olivia had grown out of accepting spontaneous motherly affection a while ago.

Olivia headed off to her room and banged the door shut behind her.

Happy times at the Steele-Ferros.

✳ ✳ ✳

Micky never visited The Pink Bean before lunch, and the morning rush took her by surprise. She watched as Kristin and Josephine, the only other morning-shift employee, moved behind the counter with astounding efficiency. As a mother who had just fought with her daughter over bathroom time, Micky greatly doubted her ability to ever do what the two women were accomplishing. They had a rhythm about them, Kristin taking the orders and Josephine executing them seamlessly.

Micky felt foolish just standing around like that. The only thing she'd done so far was take cups of coffee to customers who were sitting at a table, but at this time of the day, most beverages were sold for on-the-go.

Another conclusion she drew was that by opening The Pink Bean, Kristin had built a goldmine. Australians were serious about their coffee, and they were equally willing to pay good money—albeit way too much—for a cup of it from their favorite vendor. Micky imagined all the people who had walked out of there with a scalding hot paper cup on their way to the office, enjoying Kristin's work. And it was hard work, she could see now.

"Hi, Micky," Sheryl, Kristin's partner, said. "First day, huh?" She stood in the middle of the line, clearly not expecting special treatment.

Micky walked over to her, feeling exceedingly self-conscious. She pecked Sheryl quickly on the cheek. "It's a bit daunting."

"I bet." Sheryl always dressed casually for work, and

today was no different. She wore jeans and a loose-hanging blouse. Micky actually looked forward to getting to know her and Kristin better. They were acquaintances now who said hello and good-bye to each other and had never gotten further than making small talk. They were an impressive couple to whom, Micky had to admit, she looked up.

"Why don't you sit down and I'll bring over your coffee?" Micky said.

Sheryl gave a deep belly laugh. "You obviously don't yet know the rules of The Pink Bean." She shuffled forward in the queue. "General Park over there doesn't do nepotism." She eyed her partner from a distance. "Not even for me, her wife who owns half this place." She winked at Micky. "I'll wait my turn, otherwise I'll get in trouble tonight."

Micky gave a nervous giggle. She'd know all about Kristin's rules soon enough.

She looked at the ever-growing queue and wondered what was so much better about being there than her usual routine of meandering around the aisles of the organic supermarket in Potts Point and picking out the best-looking produce for dinner—at least her children always had a huge appetite after school.

"Micky, can you fetch us some more cocoa powder from the back, please," Kristin asked, and Micky snapped to attention, though she had no idea where the cocoa powder, or anything else for that matter, was to be found.

CHAPTER THREE

It was Micky's third day on the job. She'd successfully made it through the morning rush, working the register, smiling at people, giving them back their correct change if they paid cash, and even having a brief chat with a few regulars she recognized.

She was wiping down a table when Amber walked in.

"Green tea?" Micky asked automatically. Amber didn't drink coffee, only gallons of tea.

"Yes, and a side of my best friend, please. Where were you yesterday afternoon? I thought you only worked the morning shift?"

Micky shook her head while she put a tea bag into a mug. "I was too exhausted for yoga. I'm not used to this. I've only been here two and a half hours today, and my feet are already killing me."

"You can use that as an excuse once, but not twice. You know I'm all for you having this job, but I don't want you jeopardizing your practice." Amber always referred to yoga as a *practice*.

"And suddenly I have two bosses, whereas a couple of days ago, I had none." Micky handed Amber her tea.

"Is Kristin leaving you alone in here already?"

"This is the quiet hour. Everyone's at work. Kristin has gone upstairs for a bit, and Josephine is on the phone with a supplier in the back."

"How's your new adventure going?" Amber asked in between blowing on her tea.

"It's definitely still in the challenging phase." They both

looked at the door as it opened. A woman walked in. Micky's pulse picked up speed slightly. She'd made plenty of practice-cups of coffee by now, but this would be her first time without supervision, unless the woman ordered tea like Amber—Micky hoped that she would.

"I'll leave you to it," Amber said and headed to a table by the window.

"A tall wet capp, please," the woman said.

"Excuse me?" Did this woman know she was in a coffee shop?

"My regular. A wet cappuccino." Her blue eyes seemed to look straight through Micky. If she was a regular, couldn't she see that Micky was new? Or perhaps she was one of those people who never took notice of who served them.

"I'm very sorry. I'm new here, and thus far, no one has explained to me what a wet cappuccino might be." Wasn't all coffee wet by definition?

The woman sighed audibly. *She'll roll her eyes at me next.* "Wet means a bigger ratio of milk to foam." She stood there with a massive air of superiority about her.

"So a latte?" Micky asked.

The woman did roll her eyes then. "If I wanted a latte, I would have ordered a latte." Her tone of voice was nothing like the friendly customers Micky had served throughout the morning. This woman was loud and brash and certainly didn't have an Australian accent. She sounded American, and acted like it—like she owned the bloody world.

But Micky knew she couldn't mock the customer. This was a business, and customer satisfaction was key. "That'll be three dollars ninety-nine, ma'am," she said. "Coming right up." Micky couldn't help giving the woman a defiant stare, in case she thought she didn't sound utterly ridiculous.

The woman paid cash without saying another word, then walked to the side of the counter, her heels clicking loudly, to wait for her latte—Micky refused to call it a wet cappuccino, even in her head.

Why must people be so unpleasant and have their head stuck so far up their ass, she wondered as she prepared the beverage. But this was one of the challenges that came with her brand new job: dealing with difficult customers. Micky was sure it wouldn't be her last. And if the woman was indeed a regular, Micky would be making her many more *wet cappuccinos* to come.

"Hi, Robin." Josephine sauntered out of the back door.

So she was called Robin. Without looking up from her phone, she mumbled something, reminding Micky of her son's favorite way of having a conversation with his mother —unwilling to tear his gaze away from his precious iPhone and showing her that he was actually listening to what she was saying. Micky cataloged Robin as an overly pampered expat.

"Here you go." She handed Robin her drink, their gazes crossing briefly when she did. Robin had an awfully intense stare.

"Thanks," she said, and immediately flipped the lid off her paper cup—probably to inspect the foam to milk ratio. "Please teach your new colleague how to make my wet capp properly by tomorrow, Josephine," she said, turned on her heel, and walked out the door.

"Jesus." Micky looked at Josephine. "A *wet capp*? Really?"

"It's just a latte," Josephine said matter-of-factly.

"If only I had known that before I got my head bitten off." Micky looked over at Amber, to gauge if she'd followed the conversation between her and the annoying customer.

"Why don't you take your break," Josephine said. "Rest your feet for a bit." She was at least twenty years younger than Micky, and twenty times better at her job.

✶ ✶ ✶

"Tsk. Americans," Micky hissed as she sat down opposite Amber.

Amber shot her a friendly smile. "Don't sweat it. We're

all different."

"Indeed, some of us are pompous asses." Micky rotated her ankles and relished the feeling of relief it brought.

Amber looked at her intently. "Why are you getting so upset? She was just another person ordering another cup of coffee."

Micky shrugged. "I don't like the way she spoke to me. Did you hear what she said about me to Josephine before leaving? So rude."

"Just brush it off. It comes with the job. Not everyone can be lovely and full of positive energy like me." Amber batted her lashes ostentatiously.

Micky had to smile. "She could surely benefit from one of your classes, but she probably doesn't have time. She probably has to make some other people feel bad about themselves around seven tonight."

Amber looked at her silently.

"What?" Micky asked.

"Granted, she was being a jerk, but why can't you let it go?" She narrowed her eyes, as though inspecting Micky's face in detail.

"Because I didn't start this job to be treated like dirt, while clearly she was—"

"She was hot," Amber interrupted her. "Might that have something to do with your level of upset?"

Micky arched up her eyebrows. "Excuse me?"

Amber painted a smile on her face. "Not only that, but I'm guessing that she may have reminded you of someone with the way she waltzed in here and spoke to you."

Micky couldn't follow Amber's train of thought at all.

"Demanding, busy, overly confident?" Amber continued. "Your ex-husband comes to mind."

"Nuh-uh." Micky shook her head. "Our marriage may have run its course and ended badly, but Darren is also considerate, a great father, and only half as full of himself as that woman was."

"You like the type, that's all I'm saying," Amber teased.

"Come on, Amber. She's a, er, woman."

"I do have eyes in my head. I noticed her female features."

"You keep pushing me on that, just because of one thing I said once, after too many bottles of wine." Micky knew she was making a poor attempt at embellishing things. On top of that, Amber knew her too well to let her get away with such a statement.

"This is your workplace now, so not the place to discuss this further, but we do need to have a serious conversation about this, sooner rather than later."

"Dear Amber, you're my best friend, and an excellent yoga teacher, but that doesn't make you my life coach."

"When are the kids going to their dad's?" Amber asked, undeterred.

"Day after tomorrow." Micky simultaneously dreaded and looked forward to that day of the week. She could do with a few days of peace and quiet after starting this job, but she also—always—missed them terribly. Having to shuttle her kids around between her home and her ex's was something she would always feel guilty about. None of this was their fault, yet they had to suffer because of it.

"So, Friday evening, you're coming to yoga, then to dinner at mine. We're going to have an intimate chat. It's time."

"Are you propositioning me, Amber? I didn't know you felt that way about me." Now Micky batted her lashes in an exaggerated fashion.

"Don't be silly. You're like my sister, which is why I'm the right person to confide in."

"All because of that woman and her ridiculous coffee order?" Micky used playing dumb as a defense mechanism.

"You know why," Amber said. "I have to go now."

"Back to work I go as well." They both stood, and

Amber gave Micky an extra long hug before she left.

CHAPTER FOUR

All throughout Friday evening's yoga class—the first Micky had attended all week—Micky felt ill at ease and unable to center herself. Amber had been on her case more than usual lately, what with first pushing her to get a job, then inviting her over for an *intimate* chat. Micky had no trouble talking about herself, but there were certain topics she was loath to address.

Now they were walking toward Amber's flat, past a French restaurant, then an Indian. Micky's stomach was growling because she was used to having dinner much earlier with her kids, and if they were at their dad's, she usually had dinner at the same time as well. She sure hoped Amber had already prepared the kale and quinoa salad Micky was almost certain she was going to serve, probably with a green juice on the side, instead of a much-needed glass of wine.

The Pink Bean was located about halfway between the yoga studio where Amber taught and her flat, and whereas before the place had solely inspired extreme comfort in Micky, when she walked past it now, a slew of other emotions rose to the surface. The past week, after her first day of observing and learning, she had arrived at the coffee shop at six thirty sharp every morning—preempting the need for a shower schedule at home, because she ended up leaving the house well before her children did—and worked until Alyssa came in to cover the midday shift.

After her first full week of having a job, Micky wasn't sure yet she was cut out for it. The days suddenly seemed so much shorter, and this week, when she took an afternoon nap, she actually needed it to be able to stay up until past her kids' bedtime—and make sure they turned off the light on time.

Once they'd reached Amber's apartment and Amber, as always, offered her a large glass of water without asking, Micky said, "Please tell me you have cold wine." Micky had brought a bottle, but after sitting in her bag throughout yoga, it wouldn't be chilled enough anymore to drink.

"Would I invite you over if I didn't?" Amber was already headed toward the fridge. As usual, Micky would end up drinking two thirds of the bottle, while Amber gingerly sipped from a glass that didn't seem to get empty. Amber did have to teach tomorrow, not that she would drink much more on any other evening.

"Kimberly was shamelessly flirting with you," Micky said once they'd sat down to eat and she'd felt the soothing cold balm of white wine slide down her throat.

"That might be so, but I don't date students," Amber replied quickly. She lived by so many rules, Micky sometimes wondered how she got any actual living done.

Micky shook her head. "You meet so many women every single day, some of whom are clearly very interested in you, yet you refuse to enjoy the attention they give you." Micky was glad to discuss Amber's lack of love life instead of her own.

"I know most people see it differently, but in my view, it's unethical."

"You're not teaching children. You're teaching full-grown adults how to, ultimately, bend their legs behind their ears. I really don't see what's so unethical about that."

"First, what I teach might be physical, but I do hope that for most of the people I instruct, the outcome can be felt on a spiritual level as well. Second, my reputation is very important to me. I want to start my own studio soon, and I don't want potential clients to have any false ideas about me. How I present myself and how I behave need to be aligned."

Amber was starting to lose Micky, though Micky was desperate to keep the conversation going. She was tired, and this spinach and tofu salad that Amber had served in mason jars and turned upside down in a bowl, wasn't giving her the comfort she craved from a Friday evening meal, especially after her first official workweek.

"But all you do is teach, hang out in The Pink Bean and juice bars, and make organic salads. How can you expect to meet someone?" Micky held up her hand because she wasn't finished yet. "And you refuse to go on the internet for a date."

"I'm glad you brought up the subject," Amber said, fixing her green stare on Micky. "This is exactly what I wanted to talk to *you* about."

Micky sighed. "You always do this: You never want to talk about yourself."

All Amber did was fix Micky with a strong, silent stare —as though waiting for Micky to realize that what she had just said didn't make sense and to inform Micky she knew what she was up to.

In response, Micky drank some more. The kids were at their dad's that weekend. Darren had downsized to a much smaller townhouse as well in Lavender Bay. Olivia and Christopher's school, a new one they'd had to enroll in after the summer holiday amidst major protest and long tantrums —sentiments Micky fully understood and was trying to make up for every day—was, not coincidentally, smack dab in the middle between her and Darren's new residences.

Micky could drink as much as she wanted tonight. All she had to do was hobble the few hundred feet home, and she could sleep in as long as she wanted tomorrow.

She refocused her attention on Amber. Of course she knew what she wanted to talk about, but Micky didn't have the wherewithal to devote a lot of her emotional resources to that particular subject. First and foremost, she was a mother, and she wasn't in the habit of putting herself first like that. The only time she *had* prioritized herself was when she'd asked Darren for a divorce, because, by then, in her view, there really was no other option left. She was still paying for all the consequences of that.

"Ready when you are," Amber said. "We can talk about me all of next week, if you like." She painted a smile on her lips.

"What do you want from me?" The wine Micky was knocking back steadily was making her a bit volatile.

"Did you serve anymore wet cappuccinos this week?" Amber asked, ignoring Micky's tone.

Micky huffed out a chuckle. "If you think she's so hot, why don't you ask her out? How do you even know she's"— before her divorce, Micky had never had any issues saying the word, but it never slipped off her tongue that easily anymore—"a lesbian."

"I just know. I have the most finely tuned gaydar in Darlinghurst, perhaps in all of Sydney. It's very hard to put into words, but I just know."

"Make an effort," Micky said. Why would Micky let Amber off the hook when she was about to be grilled? Amber sighed. Perhaps Amber felt the way Micky often did when she was trying to get some personal information out of her children. Trying and mostly failing. Micky had to admit it *was* exasperating. She held up her hands. "I'm sorry. I'm being difficult."

"That's okay. I never expected this conversation to be easy." Amber took a tiny sip from her wine. "But you know I'm all about finding your truth and following it. You may think all I care about is nourishing my body with healthy food and spreading the joy and benefits of yoga, but in the end, it's really all about truth." Amber clasped her hand to her chest. "About what's in here."

Micky and Amber really were the most unlikely of friends. Then again, Amber hadn't always been like this. Neither had Micky.

"Okay, yes, though that woman annoyed the shit out of me, I found her very attractive. She's one of those people probably 90 percent of all adults on the planet would find attractive, and she knows it. Big deal," Micky blurted out.

"It's not about the wet capp woman, per se, Micky," Amber said. "I know it's hard. Even though I've been out of the closet for twenty-five years, I know it's hard to be where you are now."

"I don't even know... I've never..." Micky stammered. Even though she knew what she felt stir deep inside of her, she always came up empty when she tried to put it into words.

"Correct me if I'm wrong," Amber said, "but the way I see it is that you've been married to a man for eighteen years and now you'd like to date a woman."

"It's a bit more complicated than that." Micky didn't like the defensive tone of her own voice.

"Is it, really?" Amber's piercing green eyes scrutinized her face. "When you boil it down to its essence, is it really more complicated than that?"

"Yes." Micky sighed. "I'm forty-four years old. I have two teenage children. And I've never even..." Her words stalled again.

"It doesn't matter how old you are or how many children you have. This is about you. About finding your true self. Nothing else matters."

Micky shook her head. Amber wasn't a mother. She couldn't understand. "How can I even contemplate the notion without considering what my children will think about it?"

"Don't you think they want their mom to be happy?"

That question took Micky by surprise. All her life, but especially after the divorce, Micky had poured her energy into trying to make *them* happy, which, in turn, was a great source of happiness for her. But she'd never taken the time to consider what her children actually wanted for her. They most likely wished their mother had stayed with their father. Micky had upended their lives as well.

"I'm pretty sure they'd prefer it over me being unhappy," Micky admitted.

"For the sake of argument," Amber continued, "let's leave Liv and Chris out of it for now. Let's focus on you. What do *you* want?"

What *did* she want? Darren used to ask her that question often. In the beginning out of genuine interest and once things had started to turn sour between them, with a lot of exasperation in his voice.

"I don't know." Micky tried to rely on her standard answer, though that would never fly with Amber.

"I think you do."

Micky drank again, then said, "It's just that the concept of… dating a woman is so abstract to me. I might want it quite badly, but I just can't picture it. I can't stop thinking about the consequences and about what that would make me."

Micky witnessed Amber perk up in front of her. She always did that when they reached the crux of a conversation. Amber was the kind of person who drew massive amounts of energy from getting other people to *speak their truth*—though Micky hadn't quite reached that point yet.

"What do you think it would make you?" Amber asked, elbows on the table, her gaze resting on Micky, making her uncomfortable.

Micky looked at her hands—anything to get away from Amber's stare. "A woman who has lived a lie for most of her adult life."

"That's where I think your perception lets you down, Micky. I've known you for so long. I was your bridesmaid when you married Darren, and I know with 100 percent certainty that you loved him. You were crazy about him. Your marriage was never a lie. I do, however, think you have

22

trouble accepting the possibility that now you're someone else entirely than you were back then."

"But how can a person change like that?" The crux was about to hit Micky in the head. "You're still attracted to the same sex as you've always been." It almost came out as an accusation, while it was actually a compliment.

"But everyone is different, and there's a whole spectrum of sexual attraction out there. One doesn't have to exclude the other, and I strongly believe that, over time, we all shift a little or a lot. Life is complex. Human beings are complex. Sometimes, trying to analyze it all to death is not the best way forward," Amber said.

"Have you ever felt your preference shift?" Micky asked, though she wanted to remember to question Amber about what she thought the best way forward actually was.

Amber scrunched her lips together. "Sure. I used to date stuck-up bitches who treated me like dirt, women I wouldn't even look at twice now. That preference has surely changed."

"But at least you stayed within the same sex."

"So." Amber quirked up her eyebrows. "We can theorize about this all we want—and we will—but you're going to have to take the plunge sooner rather than later. I truly think you're ready, and I do believe that I'm the person who knows you best. I know I can be pushy, and I already pushed you to take that job, because I believe it will make you grow as a person, and now I'm pushing you again."

"You are one pushy woman, Amber."

"I prefer to see myself as a gentle nudger, but, perhaps, in this case you're right. When it comes to my best friend, I think I can allow myself some liberties." Amber smiled broadly.

"How do you suggest I, er, reach the next level?" Truth be told, Micky wouldn't know what to do without a friend like Amber in this situation.

"Start by being open to the possibility. Just a small

23

change in mindset can have big consequences. People will pick up on that." Amber's eyes started sparkling. "Who knows, maybe Miss Wet Capp will even pick up on it? Though she did come across as rather self-absorbed."

"I do hope I have the good fortune of going on my very first same-sex date with someone a bit nicer."

"Would you like me to go through my big rolodex of lesbians and set you up?" Amber still had that twinkle in her eyes. "We shouldn't aim for someone you're going to fall head-over-heels with for your first. You want to test the waters a little. Confirm your suspicions and have a bit of fun while doing so."

"I need to sleep on it."

"Alternatively, you could confide in your new boss. Kristin and Sheryl must know some eligible bachelorettes."

"You're going a little too fast for me now, Amber. Slow down."

"All right." Amber winked at her and got up to fetch the bottle of wine out of the fridge.

A frisson of excitement ran up Micky's spine. Could it really be that simple?

CHAPTER FIVE

The next Monday, after having pondered Amber's words throughout the weekend, Micky had a different kind of spring in her step when she walked to The Pink Bean. Amber had been right. Micky was ready. She was nervous and scared, but she was ready. Her conversation with Amber had left her feeling like the cork had been popped from a bottle of champagne and now all these pent-up emotions came gushing out of her.

She would look at the customers differently today—with a more open attitude, as Amber had advised. Not that she expected anything to come of that, but again, as Amber had said, it was more about the feeling that came with it.

Kristin opened the shop at six and was always there when Micky arrived at six thirty. When she kissed Micky hello, a habit she had taken up from the very first day, even her boss looked different to Micky. Everyone and everything looked different.

Next, Micky wondered about Josephine. She was a PhD student at the university where Sheryl worked. Micky watched her pour milk into a steaming jar and wondered how Amber could tell whether people were gay or not. And what if they were bisexual or anywhere else on the *spectrum* she had talked about last Friday. Micky had thought about the *spectrum* a lot.

"You and Amber should come to dinner sometime soon," Kristin said fifteen minutes later, when The Pink Bean was still empty. "Sheryl and I would love to have you over."

Micky couldn't believe it. Walking in here with an open spirit had had an immediate effect. Though, of course, Kristin had probably planned to ask her all along. Still, it didn't matter to Micky. It made her feel good—like she was on the right track.

"That would be great." Micky looked at Kristin's regal posture and her upmarket clothes. Micky didn't know what a typical coffee-shop owner looked like, but if asked to conjure up the image, Kristin would be the last person she thought of. She looked more like a lady who lunched—a very smart one. "Amber is vegan, though, for your information."

"Not an issue. Quite a few of our friends are," Kristin said. "Give me a shout when Amber pops in for her daily tea, and we'll set up a date."

"Sure thing, boss." Kristin was, of course, Micky's boss, though it didn't feel that way at all. There was nothing authoritarian about her. She never raised her voice and was an expert at going with the flow, even when things got very hectic. Kristin probably knew her bed was made. A few more years of operating a coffee shop in Darlinghurst and she could retire very gracefully.

Micky had only been on the job a week, and already an entrepreneurial spirit she didn't know she possessed reared its head. What would it be like to own a place like this—and count the takings after closing time? Apart from a job when she was in college—for a degree she never used—Micky had never earned a cent. Darren had always been the breadwinner. Micky made a tiny amount at The Pink Bean, but she wasn't there for the money—although the very act of earning it felt good.

Perhaps, what it came down to was that Micky saw Kristin as a role model. She was an out lesbian with a long-term partner and her own business. She was a lot of things Micky could only dream of being. Or could she do more than dream?

* * *

After the morning rush had passed and Amber had come and gone—and a dinner date at Kristin and Sheryl's had been set up for the coming Saturday—Micky relaxed with a macchiato, leafing through a copy of *LOTL* magazine.

She had just gotten engrossed in a story about an older lesbian coming out of the closet—called a *latebian* in the article—when the door of The Pink Bean opened. Micky's reflex was to look up, and she saw it was Robin. She wasn't dressed in the pantsuit Micky had become used to seeing her in. Instead, she wore a tiny pair of shorts, long, white socks pulled up all the way to her knees and a very tight tank top. She was also covered in sweat, which made her arms glisten —and her biceps and triceps stand out in a pretty impressive manner.

Crikey.

Robin ordered her ridiculously named beverage from Josephine, and instead of waiting for it at the counter the way she always did, she sat down at the table next to Micky's.

Micky tried to focus on the article she'd been reading, but the words danced in front of her eyes. Her gaze kept being pulled to Robin's legs and the bare patch of thigh between the socks and the shorts. This woman boasted some serious muscle tone. But what was up with the socks?

"I do CrossFit," Robin said. "That's why I wear these." She patted the sock closest to Micky. "They protect my shins when I do deadlifts."

Had she been reading Micky's mind? Additionally, Robin might as well have been speaking Chinese, judging by how much of what she'd said Micky had actually understood.

"Oh," she replied, just to say something. She was also perplexed that haughty Robin would even take the time to speak to her—a lowly coffee-shop employee.

"Here you go." Josephine brought over Robin's cappuccino.

Robin thanked Josephine, stirred her coffee once, then looked at Micky. "What's your story then?"

Was she actually making conversation with Micky after having been so rude to her last week? Micky had seen her come in every day since, but as though luck itself had shone down on her, she'd never had to serve her. And what kind of a question was that? What was wrong with a simple hello, perhaps followed by a quick apology for being such an ass the other day?

Micky fixed her with a stare that, hopefully, said all she had to say. But then she remembered Kristin's words— delivered in her head in Kristin's gentle tone of voice. "The customer is always right, even if they're wrong." Micky had no choice but to be nice to her.

"Why does a woman of your age work in a place like this?" Robin didn't let up. She had the kind of voice that, Micky suspected, got a lot of things done.

"Circumstance," Micky said, but only because she had to answer something.

Not only did Robin order the most ridiculous drink, she was also wearing an insane outfit, she'd been rude to Micky without offering an apology, and the tone she addressed Micky with was hardly convivial. Micky wanted to just get up and leave. This job was supposed to empower her, not have the opposite effect.

"Ha, you're the mysterious type," Robin said. "That's okay. Color me intrigued. Will you at least tell me your name?" She had the audacity to smile seductively at Micky.

Wait. Was that really what that smile looked like?

"It's Micky." Micky's head was about to start spinning.

"Well, Micky, how about tomorrow when I come in, I ask you out? I'm giving you a heads-up because you look like the type who has to think about it for at least twenty-four hours."

Micky's jaw slacked. "What?" she managed to say after a few long, awkward seconds.

"Think about it." Robin winked, then looked away and downed her coffee in a few large gulps. When she got up, she said, "I need to hit the shower and get to work. See you tomorrow."

Micky was still recovering from what had just happened after Robin was long gone.

✶ ✶ ✶

Micky had needed the yoga class she attended with Amber the previous afternoon more than she'd ever needed it before. She had also needed Amber's advice—though she could easily predict it.

"It's a sign," Amber had said. "Take the opportunity with both hands."

"But... I can't stand the woman," Micky countered, whereupon Amber put her hands on her sides and gave Micky one of her looks.

"I think you can. Give her a chance. Perhaps she's exactly the kind of person you're looking for at this time of your life. You like loud, brash people, Micky, we both know that. You're not looking for someone else to marry at this point, however, and she's hot."

Micky shook her head in desperation. Robin asking her out might very well be a sign of something else entirely. Like letting Micky know this was a bad idea and she should get her priorities straight.

Amber grabbed her by the shoulders and said, "Go for it, Micky. I'll call you when the date is in progress so that, if you need an excuse, you can leave. I'll pretend to be Olivia."

Micky did want to go for it, but not with a CrossFitting arrogant woman like Robin. Though, as usual, there was a sliver of truth to Amber's words when she claimed that Micky liked the type. Unless she had a different taste in women than in men. She had always loved Darren's loud, look-at-me ways—an aspect of his personality that was beginning to show in Olivia. But at least Darren had never been obnoxious and he was always polite.

Then again, the fact that she was so conflicted about Robin and that she found it surprisingly hard to give her a clear no for an answer, must mean something.

So, by the time Robin entered The Pink Bean—not sporting white knee socks this time, but dressed impeccably in a navy pantsuit over a bright white blouse—and fixed her with a stare, Micky was ready to say yes. Even though she could be making the worst mistake of her life. But then, at least, she would have tried. She would have conquered some of her fear, just by saying one simple word: yes.

Robin drew her lips into a magnetic smile, giving Micky the impression that she was really turning it on for her. Perhaps she had one of those Jekyll & Hyde personalities. It did gnaw at Micky that Robin was the sort of person who could treat service personnel so rudely, without even apologizing for it. Being nice to people, in the end, didn't cost a thing. Being nasty, as Amber would say, always cost you in karma points and putting negative energy into the universe.

But, more than any of that, Micky had the strong urge to show Robin that she was so much more than a woman working in a coffee shop. Even if whatever she was trying to prove was more to herself than anyone else, she felt as though she could only accomplish that by rising to this challenge. She was skilled at hiding it, except from Amber, but Micky had suffered from issues of decreasing self-esteem since her divorce—an overall sentiment of floating on thin air and not having a clue where her life was going—and, if she was honest, the fact that someone like Robin would be interested in her, was a boost to her ego.

"Have you thought about it?" Robin asked, while she waited for her coffee.

Micky felt self-conscious standing behind the counter, with Josephine only a few feet away. She rubbed her hands on her apron. Was she really going to do this? A flare of last-minute doubts shot through her, but then she caught Robin's gaze and it was one of those looks that felt aimed at her and her alone, and made Micky feel like she was the most important woman on the planet.

"My answer is yes," she said, keeping the tremor that reverberated through her muscles out of her voice successfully. She also wanted some time alone with Robin to ask her how she had known that Micky would even be interested in going on a date with another woman. What had given her away? The magazine she'd been reading and her level of being engrossed in it? Or the simple fact that she worked at The Pink Bean and was therefore gay by association?

"Terrific." Robin looked like she'd just closed a big, long-awaited deal—the kind of smug Micky had a strange soft spot for. "Are you free this weekend?"

"Er, no." Micky had anticipated this question, and while she had no problem going to dinner at Kristin and Sheryl's during a weekend the kids were with her, she couldn't possibly go on a date with a stranger. What would she say to them? *While I was working at The Pink Bean a woman asked me out?* "I'm not actually."

"You keep intriguing me, Micky." Robin's tone became flirty. "When *are* you free?"

"Not before next Wednesday." Wednesday was switch-over day. Micky picked Olivia and Christopher up after school every other week so they wouldn't have to take the bus with their stuff, even though they had two sets of all essentials by now.

Robin chuckled. "Not tonight either?"

"Tonight?" Micky exclaimed in panic. She was free that night, but it wouldn't give her any time to mentally prepare. Maybe that was how she needed this to go, however. Given the opportunity to wait a week, and think this date to death before it had even happened, would most likely make her back out. Why not tonight? The kids were only coming back tomorrow. It would save her another lonely evening

31

watching television. "Yes, I'm free tonight."

"Excellent. I'll make a reservation at Fabio's just down the block. Shall we meet for drinks at Barrio first? Around seven thirty?"

Drinks at seven thirty? When on earth would they have dinner? Now that she worked and got up at five thirty every morning, Micky liked to be in bed by ten. But this was no time to consider sleep. Sacrifices had to be made here.

"Sounds good."

"Okay." Robin dug a hand in her blazer pocket and handed Micky a card. "Here's my number in case you need to reach me." She shot Micky another million-dollar smile.

Micky stared at the card in her hands, then back at Robin. She didn't have a business card of her own to hand out.

"I need to get to the office now. Looks like I'll be knocking off early tonight." She winked at Micky. She retrieved her takeaway coffee from the counter, turned, and left.

"Did I hear that correctly?" Josephine whispered. "Are you going out with the alpha?"

The alpha? Micky couldn't think of a better description herself. "Looks like I am."

"Good on ya, Micky." Josephine nodded approvingly. "Truth be told, I didn't even know you were batting for our team, but I guess working here and all, it makes sense now."

Micky didn't reply. Her brain was busy dealing with the consequences of being rocked out of her post-divorce lull and trying to process she was going on a date with Robin. She looked at the card in her hand. Robin Mortimer. Regional Diversity Manager for Asia Pacific, it said. Obviously she worked for Goodwin Stark, one of the big banks. Thank goodness not NPBC, where Darren worked. What did a diversity manager even do? She would have ample opportunity to find out tonight.

Shit. Tonight.

CHAPTER SIX

Micky had hesitated between going to yoga and getting a pep talk from Amber or taking a much-needed afternoon nap, what with the prospect of staying up past her bedtime that night. She'd opted for the nap, only to find herself tossing and turning, her mind unable to relax, her heart beating in her throat with nerves. Was she really doing this? Or was she simply losing her mind?

The afternoon passed painfully slowly, but then, when the time came to get ready, she didn't know where it had gone. She could have used another few days to get herself—and her mindset—ready for this. What had she said to Amber the other day? *I do hope I have the good fortune of going on my very first same-sex date with someone a bit nicer.* And here she was. Deciding what to wear to meet Robin Mortimer. The whole thing was ludicrous.

She glanced at her reflection in the mirror and, out loud, said, "I should cancel."

She looked around for her phone and Robin's card. It would be so easy to send a text message. It would all be over and done with. And then what? Everything would go back to being normal. Wasn't that exactly what Micky was trying to escape? She knew it was just fear holding her back at this point. First-date jitters as well, of course. Micky's last first date was more than twenty years ago, when Darren had asked her out. When she came to think of it, something she hadn't done in a long time, the way Darren had approached her was not unlike Robin had.

Micky had been helping out at a student union party.

She was pulling beers behind the bar when this cocky guy came up to her and said, "I don't care that you're selling them. I'm buying you a beer."

"I don't drink beer," Micky had protested, even though she did. She just didn't want to give him the satisfaction of easily complying.

"Then let me take you out for a nice bottle of wine. How does tomorrow evening sound?"

Was she attracted to Robin because she was a female version of her ex-husband, despite the appalling way in which they'd met? Micky was no psychiatrist, but she reasoned that she might be looking for something familiar to hold on to.

Micky snapped to, chasing the memory of Darren from her mind, and refocused on the blouse she had pulled from her closet. If she wanted to cancel, she would have to do so right then. Any later would make it very impolite—or perhaps more plausible that she had an emergency. Micky had two children. She always had an excuse.

"I'm going on this date," she said to herself, watching her lips move in the mirror. "Fuck it. I'm doing it."

★ ★ ★

Robin was dressed in jeans and a white blouse with pink vertical stripes. Micky was only two minutes late, but Robin had obviously arrived a while ago because a half-empty bottle of red wine stood in front of her.

Robin rose when she saw her and pecked Micky on the cheek.

"Did I get the time wrong?" Micky asked.

"Nope. I just like to arrive early." Was that a hint of kindness in Robin's eyes?

Micky sat down, desperately wanting—needing—some of that wine. "What are you drinking?"

"A heavenly Barossa Shiraz from the year 2012." Robin seemed to know her wines. "Australian wines can be quite spectacular. Mind you, after five years in Singapore and

Hong Kong, where they charge you an arm and a leg for the export bin stuff, I'm easily pleased." She started looking around for a waiter. "Want to try?" She offered Micky her glass.

"Er, sure." Micky grabbed the glass and sipped gingerly. "It won't be a hardship to have a glass of that."

Robin asked the waiter for an extra glass, then poured Micky a generous portion. When she held up her glass, she said, "I honestly didn't think you'd say yes, what with the way I spoke to you that day." She pinned her blue gaze on Micky. "Are you planning any kind of payback for that?"

"Still contemplating it," Micky said in a, to her surprise, flirty tone. She didn't know she had it in her. "Still waiting for an apology as well."

Robin leaned over the table a little. "I'm really sorry. I could try to come up with a bunch of excuses, but there really are none for behavior like that. But, just so you know, I don't go about my day being condescending to people. That's not what I do at all."

"All right." Micky was glad this particular patch of air was cleared between them. "What does a Diversity Manager do, anyway?"

Robin held up a finger. "I'll tell you all about it in a minute, but I just need to know that I'm forgiven." She held out her glass. "Clink if I am." She cocked her head.

Granted, Micky didn't have any experience at all when it came to flirting with women, but Robin was turning it on for sure.

Micky bumped the belly of her wine glass against Robin's. "I wouldn't be here if I hadn't been able to look past your blatant arrogance."

"Which makes you a wiser woman than me, though, to my credit, my arrogance allowed me to ask you out, so there's that."

A few minutes into this date and Micky had had more fun than she'd had in the past year. There was something in the air between them; she could clearly feel it now. That's why she had said yes and refrained from canceling. Her subconscious had known. At least, that's how Amber would put it.

"I just have a thing for arrogance. It's my fatal flaw." Micky could turn it on as well, it appeared.

"Lucky me then." Robin chuckled.

A short silence fell between them. Too short to be uncomfortable. Just a little breathing room.

"About my job," Robin said. "I'm tasked with making sure everyone in the company gets the same chances. Not just the straight white dudes."

"That must be quite the challenge in the industry you're in." Throughout her marriage to Darren, Micky had sat through many a stiff dinner with a bunch of white *dudes*, all deeming themselves more important than the other, testosterone brimming in their eyes. Micky hated those dinners.

"Let's just say I'm the right woman for the job. It's easier in Australia. This is supposed to be my last stop before I head back to New York. Try creating a diverse workforce in conservative Singapore and narrow-minded Hong Kong. Now that was a challenge."

Robin told Micky about the overprivileged *wanker bankers* in Hong Kong and how being a female banker there basically equaled not having a family because the work hours were crazy. The more she talked, the more fascinating Micky found her.

"But enough about me," Robin said after a while. "Tell me about you."

"My story is much less interesting, I'm afraid," Micky said, then her phone rang. She'd completely forgotten about Amber's promise to call. "Oh, sorry about that." She pressed the *Ignore* button.

"A friend checking up on you?" Robin had a smile on her face. She must go on plenty of dates to so swiftly conclude that.

"Busted." Micky smiled back, and it felt as though the combination of their smiles ignited something in her belly.

"At least you're not picking up. I'll take it as a compliment." Robin finished the last of her wine. "Shall we move on to dinner, where you can tell me all about yourself?"

Micky nodded, not experiencing any signs of fatigue. The first leg of the date couldn't have gone better, and she was curious what the rest of the night had in store for her.

★ ★ ★

Robin's eyes grew wide. "You've never been with a woman." She repeated what Micky had just hesitatingly admitted in a bit too loud a voice for Micky's comfort. The restaurant they were at was cozy but tiny, and it was easy to overhear the other patrons.

Micky didn't know what to say next.

Robin seemed to recover from the shock quite quickly. "It's strange, because I really got the vibe off you, and well, you said yes to the date." She bit her lip for an instant. "I take it you are interested in me, because if you think you're not, I may have to tell you something you don't want to hear." She followed up with a smile Micky couldn't immediately decipher.

"The very fact that I'm sitting here means I'm interested," Micky said curtly. So far, she'd enjoyed the increasingly flirty vibe between them. But now that the conversation had flowed back to this crucial fact about her, she was feeling uncomfortable again. As though she had to defend herself for the course her life had taken.

"I was right to be intrigued by you." Robin turned up the wattage of her smile. "It's okay, Micky. I just wasn't expecting it, but I can definitely work with what you've just told me."

What did that even mean? Was that some lesbian code Micky wasn't yet privy to? Micky couldn't possibly consider herself a lesbian. Or maybe she was a "latebian," like the woman she'd been reading about in that magazine when Robin had started talking to her.

"I also have two children in their teens." Micky might as well tell it all right then, though she categorically refused to ever feel the slightest bit uncomfortable when it came to her offspring. If that was some sort of deal breaker for Robin, so be it. The date would end there and then.

Robin just nodded, dropped her fork, and refilled their wine glasses. "Here's how I see it," she said after taking a long gulp. Micky hadn't held back on downing the drinks either, and she was starting to dread the sound of her alarm clock in the morning. "You are looking for your first experience, and well, at the risk of sounding extremely blasé, though we've already kind of established that's part of the attraction," Robin put her hand on the table, "you've found the right woman for that introduction." Her hand scooted closer to Micky's. "I'm not looking for anything serious. I'm simply not the type. I'm looking for a good time, and I think, Micky, that you and I could have a really good time together. No strings attached." Robin's fingers caressed Micky's knuckles. "What do you think?"

Robin's ever-so-slight touch was making Micky's head spin. Her words didn't really register, though Micky got the gist of them. She mainly focused on the no-strings-attached bit.

"I will gladly be your starter woman," Robin added, then curled her fingers around Micky's wrist.

There's arrogance and then there's this. But inside, Micky warred with her obvious attraction to Robin, and all that had just been said. Micky wasn't exactly looking for anything serious either. She was just… looking. But could she really be coldly pragmatic about this? Because what Robin was doing, if she was reading this situation right, was blatantly propositioning her.

"I'm going to have to think about that." Micky bought

herself some time. "Perhaps over a second date."

A waitress approached their table. "Can I interest you ladies in the dessert menu?" She didn't seem to notice that Robin's fingers were curled around Micky's wrist, but her sudden presence made Micky break out into a cold sweat.

Micky didn't know if she wanted to flee the scene and process this date in tipsy solitude, or prolong it and see what would happen.

"We'll have a look," Robin said, and only removed her fingers when the waitress handed them the menus.

It was as though Micky could only then take a deep breath and try to find a little of her old self again. But there was also that instant desire to feel Robin's hand on hers again.

"I'm not really hungry anymore," Micky said, looking into Robin's eyes.

"My place is very close. We can have a nightcap there." Robin's stare was unwavering.

If Micky hadn't been sitting, she surely would have gone weak at the knees. Was this really happening? She could hardly ask if Robin was suggesting a one-night stand, but that was how Micky was interpreting the situation. Was she even considering it? Was she that sort of person? Figuring out what kind of person she was had been part of the purpose of this date. Micky tried to conjure up Amber's voice. She should go to the bathroom and call her, ask for her best friend's advice. But this wasn't up to Amber. It was high time for Micky to start making her own decisions anyway. What this particular decision boiled down to at this very moment was how attracted she was to Robin and how much she wanted to be with her.

An undeniable amount, Micky concluded. "Okay," she said, and sealed her fate.

CHAPTER SEVEN

On the way to her apartment, Robin had made small talk, and Micky had nervously tried to engage in it, but so much was running through her head. If she was actually going to go through with this, she would need that nightcap.

"Whiskey, brandy, or something sweeter?" Robin asked after escorting Micky up to her loftlike home.

"The stronger, the better." Micky was holding on to the back of a chair while looking around the place, but automatically, her gaze was pulled back to Robin.

Robin smiled and took a step in her direction. "It's perfectly normal to be nervous." Then she leaned over and whispered in Micky's ear, "As long as you're also very aroused."

Arousal wasn't the problem. In some shape or form, Micky had been dreaming about a moment like this for a very long time. But, perhaps, she had hoped for a bit more romance to accompany it. For it to mean something more in the end than this ever could. She remembered Amber's words. *You're not looking for someone else to marry at this point.* Micky gave an uncomfortable chuckle.

"We *can* have a second date." Robin raised her voice back to speaking level. "There's no rush, no obligations, no expectations." She grabbed for Micky's hand again. "I want you to be comfortable and, more than anything, to enjoy yourself."

The hand grab, and how it shot an arrow of pure, unmistakable lust up Micky's spine, made her decide. Why not have her first time with a woman be with someone as sure of herself as Robin?

Micky reached for Robin's neck and pulled her close. "I want you," she said. "Forget about the drink. Take me to bed."

Robin put her free hand on the back of Micky's head and kissed her on the lips.

Despite having imagined a moment like this a million times, and for much longer than Micky felt comfortable admitting to herself, this was the first time Micky's lips had met another woman's in a kiss. And what a woman Robin was. There was strength in the grasp of her hands around Micky's neck, but also tenderness.

Micky remembered how ridiculous she believed Robin to have looked in her CrossFit socks, but realized now that, more than ridiculous, Robin had looked smoking hot. Now, Micky was about to lay eyes and hands on that smoking hot body.

She pushed any thoughts of work, of having to get up early and the consequences of what she was doing, to the back of her mind and, finally, let loose and enjoyed the kiss.

For Micky, that meant pressing her body against Robin's and allowing the gentle, close-lipped pecks they'd been exchanging to turn into much more. Micky's tongue greeted Robin's, and when it did, she briefly opened her eyes. Perhaps to check in with herself, assess whether she really wanted this—oh yes!—or perhaps just to catch a glimpse of Robin, who had turned out to be quite a different kind of person than Micky had believed her to be based on first assumptions.

"Come on," Robin said, when their lips parted. She shot Micky a narrowed-eyed smile, and Micky went all warm inside.

Micky followed Robin into the bedroom, which to Micky's relief, was a room with actual walls. But Micky was no longer interested in decorations and interior design. She only had eyes for Robin, who was coming for her again, wrapping her hands around Micky's neck, pulling her in.

The kiss that followed reached Micky somewhere deep inside, in a spot that hadn't tingled like that in years. It wasn't just the fact that, somehow, she had full confidence in Robin and what she was doing, but even more so that Micky was standing in another woman's bedroom, kissing her. It had been a long time coming. Even though this particular night had come out of the blue.

Oh Christ, what was Micky doing? Why couldn't she get her brain to shut up? She wanted to enjoy every single second of this. Her first time with a woman would only happen once.

When they broke from the kiss, Micky took a step back.

"Are you all right?" Robin asked. If there was any worry in her glance, it was veiled by a look of pure lust.

Micky sighed. "I'm sorry. I guess I'm a little overwhelmed by the situation. This is, er, my first—"

Robin bridged the distance between them. "You're in good hands, Micky," she said, then found Micky's ear again, "even if I do say so myself." She followed up with a short giggle. "Just relax and have a good time." Robin stood up straight and looked Micky in the eye. "I want you too," she said, and her voice had gone all low, the tone and desire in it connecting with Micky's core.

She nodded, small slow nods at first, but quickly turning them into confident ones. Micky inhaled deeply, the way Amber had taught her to do before every meeting with her divorce lawyer—in through the nose, out through the mouth.

"I'm ready," she said. And she was. One year after the divorce had been finalized, Micky was ready.

Robin sank her teeth into her bottom lip and stood there, scrutinizing Micky a few moments longer, then nodded back at her. In one swift movement, without unbuttoning it, she pulled her blouse over her head and stood in front of Micky in her bra.

Jesus. Micky had had a hint of what lay beneath—and of how amply Robin's blouse had been filled out—but now that she came face to face with the evidence, she felt something throb between her legs. Micky quickly came to the conclusion that yoga was no match for CrossFit—and the fact that Micky had given birth twice didn't help with her confidence either.

Not only could Micky actually see the outline of Robin's abs as she stood there, with her arms on her sides, waiting for Micky to, perhaps, mirror what she had just done and start stripping, but Robin had an insanely toned set of arms on her as well. This woman was a goddess—and way out of Micky's league, though she had no idea who would be within her divorced, mother-of-two, never-been-with-a-woman range.

"You... are..." Micky stuttered. She was aroused, oh yes, but also too intimidated to speak, let alone pull her top over her head.

Robin took a step toward her. "And you are beautiful," she said, her voice serious. "And you need to get out of your head." She kissed Micky gently on the cheek. When she started to undo the buttons of Micky's blouse, Micky couldn't keep her eyes off Robin's upper arms. "Let me help you with that." Robin slipped Micky's blouse off her shoulders, and before Micky had the chance to even start feeling self-conscious, she ran her hands over Micky's sides, flooding her with lust instead of self-doubt. "Let me take care of everything," Robin continued. She unsnapped Micky's pants next while peppering her neck with kisses, her breath hot on Micky's skin.

Robin easily kneeled and tugged Micky's pants off her, getting rid of her shoes in the process. Every time Micky caught sight of Robin's gorgeous body and tempting smile, she felt a little less self-conscious because desire was starting to get the upper hand. Micky had only waited her entire adult life for this moment. A moment she had long believed she would never experience. Besides, Micky took good care of herself and there was no use comparing the state of her body to someone who was clearly a great deal younger *and* a fitness fanatic.

Robin had asked her out and brought her here. Surely a few stretch marks weren't going to make the difference now.

"May I?" Robin asked, and brought her hands behind Micky's back.

Having Robin's hands all over her made Micky's breath come faster, and she panted a little when she gave Robin permission to unhook her bra.

Then there she stood. Naked but for a pair of underwear in Robin's bedroom. Micky had no more considerations about how odd life can be or any of that. Her mind was saturated with other thoughts. The first and foremost issue at hand was getting Robin's bra off. But Micky didn't have to lift a finger. Robin was doing all the work, giving Micky the opportunity to shamelessly gawk at her very gawk-worthy body.

Micky did make a mental note to later ask why Robin had asked her out. Why Micky Ferro of all the women in Sydney? But that thought soon got pushed to the side as Robin let her bra drop to the floor.

Micky's mouth started watering. Robin's breasts were so perfect that Micky's first thought was whether they were real, then that thought was substituted by the prospect of touching said breasts with her very hands, her lips, her tongue. Micky's insides were smoldering with a desire she had pushed away for too long. But this was it. This was happening. One-night stand or not, no strings attached or not, after this night, Micky's life would be forever altered. She would be a new woman.

After she got rid of her jeans and she was just as scarcely dressed as Micky, Robin pulled Micky onto the bed with her. When their skin met as they tumbled onto the mattress, more fire ignited in Micky's belly. She was all in now. She was ready to cast away the most persistent doubts, fears, and everything else that had held her back for so long. In this bed, Micky was not a divorced mother. She was a woman truly finding herself for the first time in her life.

Robin slipped on top of her, kissed her neck, her cheek, her jaw, then her lips for long, long moments, while her hands let loose in Micky's hair, and her knee pressed against her panties.

Micky rode the wave of sensory overload happily. Despite her hard muscles, everything about Robin was so soft. Her touch insistent but light as a feather, her skin taut but smooth.

Micky's breath came faster as Robin's caresses intensified. Micky let her own hands roam across Robin's back, digging her fingertips into her flesh, pushing her pelvis against Robin's knee. Oh, what it would feel like when her panties came off.

Micky would have to wonder about that a little while longer while Robin took her sweet time kissing every inch of Micky's belly before stopping and gazing down at her breasts.

Ever so slowly, on those strong arms of hers, Robin lowered herself until her mouth was hovering over Micky's nipple, then she planted the most gentle of kisses on it. In response, Micky's skin turned into a plane of goose bumps. Good God. If she wasn't actually there witnessing this, feeling this, Micky wouldn't believe it was really happening. The effect of just a small touch of lips on her nipple. How was it possible to feel so much from that?

Robin repeated the action on Micky's other nipple, and again the sensation shot through her like an arrow made of liquid lust. The entire expanse of Micky's skin was throbbing now. But Robin was far from finished with bestowing attention on her breasts.

Robin's hard nipples pressed into the flesh of her belly,

while Robin let her tongue dart around Micky's nipples and sucked them into her mouth.

An involuntary moan escaped Micky's mouth. Her entire body was turning into desire. Micky was being reduced to just pure want, raw lust, and the excruciating desire for Robin to rip her panties off and do what she was going to do.

It felt as though Robin was all over her, kissing her everywhere at once, while she kneaded her breasts, grasped her buttocks, and now... Oh, now Robin's hands were dangerously close to Micky's panties. Micky couldn't take it anymore. She brought her own hands to her panties and, together with Robin, pushed them off her, baring herself.

As if by instinct, and as though this was all she'd ever done in life, Micky's knees fell wide, allowing Robin to take in every last inch of her. Robin's gaze on her body aroused Micky beyond belief. The desire coursing through her was unparalleled. All of this was new, but felt so familiar at the same time—so right.

For a brief moment, Robin painted a small but wicked grin on her lips, then she ducked between Micky's legs. She kissed Micky's inner thighs; she kissed the line of skin above her pubic hair, then let her lips wander down.

Micky's muscles tensed with anticipation. This goddess of a woman was about to go down on her. Just the thought of it happening, seconds before it actually did, made Micky's pussy lips pulse wildly. The pulse seized her entire body. Micky had been reduced to one giant pulsing mess of extreme need.

Robin inched her lips closer to Micky's pussy. Then... touchdown. It was soft and excruciating and exhilarating all at the same time. Most of all, it was the most erotic sensation Micky had ever experienced. Lying in Robin's bed like this, spread wide for her, with Robin skating her tongue along her lips. It was also almost unbearable. So much heat and pleasure traveled through Micky's flesh. It was just too much. Soon, it would all erupt.

Robin danced her tongue around Micky's clit while—oh goodness—she circled a finger around the entrance of Micky's pussy. Robin slipped her finger inside, high and deep, while she kept dancing her tongue about.

Then it all came crashing down.

Years of pent-up lust, of denied emotions, of unmet desire exploded out of Micky in a series of high-pitched groans. Her muscles cramped, her toes curled, and her belly tingled with the most exquisite fire.

"Oh fuck," Micky said when she came to.

Robin wiped her mouth with the back of her hand and climbed up to her. "I guess you really needed that, huh?" She had a silly smirk on her face.

"You have no idea." Micky was finally able to fully relax, her head sinking into the pillow, as she looked into Robin's face. Who would have thought that the woman who had spoken to her in such a rude manner would, only a week later, be giving her this sort of pleasure? Life was funny that way.

Micky should be exhausted, what with that obliterating climax just having taken the last of her energy, but she felt as though she could do this all night long. Yes, she had to get up early for work the next day—a blessing and a curse right then—but pouring people coffee wasn't exactly rocket science.

Robin kissed her on the cheek, then on the nose, and Micky could smell her intimate aroma on Robin's lips. This night was far from over. They'd already sort of agreed it would be a one-night stand, so Micky had to make the most of it. She was not leaving this bed before she'd had a taste of Robin.

"Don't feel as though you have to," Robin said, when Micky wiggled her way from underneath Robin's toned body.

"Try to stop me," Micky replied, emboldened by the orgasm she had just experienced, and spurred on by getting another good glimpse of Robin's *hot bod*. Who in their right mind wouldn't want to run their hands and lips all over that?

Robin scrunched her lips together and nodded. "I wouldn't dare."

Micky looked into her eyes and wondered how she would react the next time Robin came into The Pink Bean and ordered her wet cappuccino. Micky certainly wouldn't be able to serve it to her with a straight face—she'd probably burst out into a chuckle at hearing the word *wet*. All jokes aside, and having laid their cards on the table from the very beginning, Micky did like Robin a lot. She liked her easy confidence that bordered on arrogance, but also the tenderness with which she had coaxed that orgasm from her, and the banter they had engaged in before. And this body. Good grief. Not even in her wildest dreams had Micky ever imagined finding herself in bed with a woman like this.

Micky ran a finger around Robin's belly button, then dragged it up to in between her breasts. Again, while admiring their perfect shape, she wondered if they were entirely natural, but there was no sign of scars, and when pressed against her earlier, they had felt very soft and natural. She traced her finger up the slope of one breast and circled it around Robin's nipple.

Between her legs, Micky went wet like a river again. Oh, to have the weekend to explore Robin to the fullest. Yes, an entire weekend, two full days, that sounded good. Should she suggest that later? Or would Robin not be up for that? She guessed that would depend on Micky's upcoming performance.

Speaking of, Micky took Robin's perfect nipple in her mouth, and as she did, her own arousal grew bigger once again. This was no time for performance anxiety, though Micky guessed it was only normal for her to feel a bit nervous. Should she ask Robin what she liked? Robin hadn't asked her, but she had experience on her side. Micky couldn't imagine asking Robin that. She would have to trust her gut—and do what she'd imagined doing many a time.

As hard as it was to tear herself away from kissing Robin's breasts, from the way her own clit was throbbing, Micky derived it was time to go in search of Robin's. She kissed her way down Robin's belly, around her belly-button, migrating to her inner thighs, repeating what Robin had, with great success, done to her.

Once she was settled between Robin's legs, and looking —really looking—at a woman's private parts for the very first time in her life, swoop after swoop of desire rushing through her, Micky strangely felt as though she was exactly where she needed to be. This was it. She had arrived.

She kissed Robin's outer lips, slowly moving inward, and trailing her tongue along her inner lips. Robin's musky, earthy scent threw her a bit at first, until it became intoxicating and Micky started to lose track of what she was doing exactly. It was as though her tongue had taken over from her brain, and she licked and sucked, and to her great relief, Robin was squirming underneath her.

When Micky paused to catch her breath, Robin grabbed her hand and found her gaze. "Fuck me," she said. Two short words with a grand effect on Micky. A fresh wave of arousal shot through Micky, while she brought her hand to Robin's pussy. Licking Robin had been one thing—a glorious, exquisite thing—but to be inside her would be reaching another level of divine bliss.

Micky watched as one of her fingers disappeared inside of Robin, marveled at the wonder of it. Robin reacted instantly, groaning a little louder and, in between, murmuring, "More, more."

So Micky gave her more. She fucked Robin with three fingers and watched, in wonder, the effect her very fingers were having on her.

"Lick me," Robin urged.

Micky quickly complied, grateful for Robin's instructions. She stroked deep inside of Robin while she let her tongue dart around her clit. It was one of the most amazing experiences of Micky's life. To do that to another woman. To have another woman spasming with pleasure at the touch of her fingers and tongue. Micky was ready to quit her job at The Pink Bean tomorrow, if only she could repeat this a few more times.

"Oh, Micky," Robin moaned. "Oh, yes." Robin's inner walls clamped around Micky's fingers, sucking them deep inside of her.

Micky was so overwhelmed and aroused by everything that was happening that she felt she was right there with Robin, riding the height of her climax. Because it was her, Micky Ferro, having this effect on another woman, making her come at her fingertips. Micky knew there and then that this very act was the most powerful aphrodisiac she would ever encounter.

Instinctively, she knew when to withdraw, and let her fingers slide out of Robin. They were a wet and sticky mess, and Micky had no idea what to do with them.

But Robin urged her to come up. "Come here," she said. Micky had no choice but to plant her wet hand on Robin's sheets, probably leaving a nice memento.

"Not bad for a beginner," Robin said and kissed her on the cheek.

Micky didn't know what to say to that. She had many answers at the ready—"Just following your expert example." "We'll have to do that again some time very soon." "I'm so so wet again."—but she didn't utter any of them, because she questioned their appropriateness. She was also riding a wave of extreme satisfaction at what had just taken place.

No one could ever take away her first time with a woman. She also knew it wouldn't be her last.

Robin pulled Micky into a hug and whispered, "Trust me, I could do this all night long, but it's late, and we have work in the morning."

"Hm," Micky groaned, wondering if it was all right for

her to stay, but too lazy to ask. If Robin was the kind of person who wanted her to leave after what they'd just done, she would have to tell her very clearly. Micky just sank into her embrace, and then she knew she was welcome to stay. "And you have to do CrossFit," she said, just to make conversation and keep her mind off the ungodly hour she would have to ask Robin to set the alarm.

"It's past midnight, I've done my exercise for the day," Robin said, a smile in her voice.

CHAPTER EIGHT

Micky woke with a start. What time was it? Where the hell was she? Then she heard rhythmic breathing beside her and, in a flash, remembered everything that had happened. She searched for an alarm clock and found one on Robin's side of the bed. It was five fifteen. She would have to get up soon. Argh. Could she call in sick during her second week? Even though Micky had never held a proper job in her life, she did possess a certain work ethic.

She let herself fall back onto the mattress for five more minutes. But she had to go by her house and grab some clean clothes before going to The Pink Bean—and had working there not already served its purpose? Micky couldn't wait to tell Amber about this, but chances were that, by the time Amber came to the coffeehouse for her daily green tea, Micky would be snoozing in the storeroom.

"Morning," Robin said, her voice croaky. "Do you have to get up already?" She threw an arm over Micky's middle, trapping her in the bed.

"I have to be there at six thirty and go by my house first." Should Micky have prepared for this scenario and put a spare pair of underwear in her bag? This made her wonder if Robin was the kind of person who went through life with a clean pair of panties tucked away in her purse. There was so much Micky didn't know about Robin, and would probably never find out.

"I'll lend you a pair of panties," Robin mumbled. She sounded as though she was still half asleep. "Stay a while longer." She snuggled up to Micky a little closer.

"I can't work in the shoes I was wearing last night."

Robin started stirring more beside her. Then she pushed herself up on one elbow and looked at Micky. "Sorry, I'm not used to waking at an ungodly hour like this. I often have conference calls with the US in the evening so I tend to go to the office late." She yawned without holding a hand in front of her mouth. "Coffee?"

"I have plenty of that at The Pink Bean." Micky smiled —she couldn't help it. Robin looked so different from last night. Still hot, but also very disheveled and a lot less arrogant. "Why don't you go back to sleep." She wanted to chat more, but this was not the time. She also needed to process. Additionally, she didn't want to make Robin feel as though she owed her in some way. If it was Robin's intention to walk away, to truly have this be a one-night stand, then Micky wasn't sure she should argue with that. Micky wasn't sure of a lot of things, apart from the fact she'd had a wild and supremely satisfying time last night. She had to speak with Amber.

"I'll see you for coffee later." Robin pressed a kiss on Micky's arm and let her head fall back onto the pillow. "I had a great time last night."

"Me too." Micky kissed Robin's hair and slipped out of bed.

★ ★ ★

Micky's body was tired, but her brain was super alert. She'd been serving customers for half an hour when, during a brief quiet spot in the morning rush, Josephine elbowed her in the side and asked, "And? How was your hot date?"

Just then, Kristin joined them behind the counter.

Micky's ears grew warm. She hoped the blush wouldn't reach her cheeks any time soon.

"You know Robin, right?" Josephine, with all her unbridled youthful enthusiasm, said to Kristin. "The hot blonde who always asks for a wet cappuccino instead of a latte?" Then she waggled her eyebrows suggestively.

"Wow, Micky." Kristin cocked her head. "That must have been one wild night. You look a bit worse for wear."

Micky hadn't had a chance to say one word about this yet. On the one hand, she was glad because she feared she might sound like a schoolgirl with a crush, but on the other hand, she did want to have a say in the matter.

"It was a good date," she said, understating it gravely. What time did Amber's morning yoga class finish again?

"It looks to me as though someone got lucky." Josephine just wouldn't leave it be. "She is so hot, Micky. Way to go."

The heat did spread over Micky's cheeks now. She wasn't even out. The gayest public thing about her up until yesterday was that she was always hanging out with Amber.

Luckily, three customers walked in at the same time, and everyone behind the counter snapped to attention.

Micky was far from comfortable having her lesbian virginity taken and then having to discuss it profusely with the people she worked with.

✳ ✳ ✳

By the time Amber arrived at The Pink Bean, Micky was exhausted, but she had hours to go before her shift ended. Still, it was good to see Amber's friendly face.

"I bet you have a lot to talk about, huh?" Josephine said. That girl. She was twenty years younger than Micky, yet spoke to her like they were best friends. "Go. Take your break." At least she was smart enough to know that Micky really needed the break.

Micky was also antsy because between nine and nine thirty was usually the time when Robin came in. She would be able to deal so much better with all of this after a good night's sleep—or at the very least an afternoon nap. But today was also the day she picked up Olivia and Christopher from school, which led her to the conclusion that, even if Robin did want to see Micky again, they'd have to wait until next week.

Micky brought over Amber's green tea—and another double espresso for herself.

"It was amazing," was the first thing she said. "My God, Amber, I feel like a different person. I'm tired and overwhelmed, and I'm pretty sure she won't want to see me again, but still, it was A-mazing." Micky was so glad she could utter these words to her best friend. Most of the tension slipped off her—making her feel even more tired.

Amber nodded. "That's so great." She wasn't the type to say I told you so. "Why do you think she won't want to see you again?"

"Erm, let's see… Divorced mother of two who has never been with another woman meets incredibly hot expat banker who's not looking for anything serious. Not exactly a match made in heaven."

"I'm not saying you should marry her, but you know, you can be friendly with each other."

"I sure wouldn't mind spending another night with her," Micky blurted out. She knocked back her espresso. This combination of feeling so wired while being bone-tired would soon catch up with her.

Then the front door opened and there she was. All freshly washed and suited up. Robin just gestured at Josephine behind the counter, then came over to Micky and Amber.

"Hi, ladies." She painted a grin on her face.

Micky was momentarily stunned but then found the wherewithal to introduce Robin to Amber and vice versa.

"Do you want that to go or to stay, Robin?" Josephine shouted from behind the counter.

"To stay, please," she said, causing a flood of relief to wash over Micky. "Do you mind if I join you?" Gosh, someone had suddenly become very polite. Maybe Robin was nervous about this as well.

"I'm just going to powder my nose." Amber rose, taking her tea with her.

Why was this so mortifying? They were all adults. Why couldn't they all just say what was what? Robin certainly hadn't had a problem with that last night.

Micky mouthed "Thank you" to her friend, then tried to look at Robin but found that, when she did, it made her go all gooey on the inside.

"Look," they both said at the same time.

But Micky was keen to let Robin do the talking, lest she say something she shouldn't.

"I meant what I said this morning," Robin went on, unperturbed. "I had a great time last night."

Just then, Josephine brought over Robin's beverage, creating another uncomfortable silence.

"Me too," Micky said as soon as Josephine left. Thank goodness there was another customer and she didn't hang around. Micky would have given a lot to have this conversation in private and not with Amber lurking a few tables away—and not at her place of work.

"Would you like to do it again some time?" Robin asked.

Micky's heart leaped into her throat. "Er, well, uh, yes," she stammered, "but I thought—"

"We can be friends with benefits," Robin added.

Coincidentally, Micky knew what that meant. She'd been ironing in the living room one evening while Olivia was watching a silly rom com with exactly the same title. They'd had a conversation about it afterward. Friends with benefits? Really?

"Okay." The hesitation in Micky's voice was unmistakable.

"We should talk about this some more in a different setting." Robin sipped from her coffee. "But the idea is to keep it casual. I don't think either one of us is in a place right now to want more." She fixed Micky with a stare that made her heart beat faster. "When can we talk properly? I'm sorry, but I need to get to work." She sipped from her coffee again, suddenly in a hurry. Maybe it was being confronted with Micky in the clear light of day that was spooking her. "You know what? You have my number. Text me?"

Robin rose, drained the last of her cup—she always drank her coffee so fast—looked at Micky funnily for a second, as though deciding whether to kiss her or not, but then clearly decided against it.

"Sure. I'll call you."

"Great." Robin quickly patted her on the shoulder, went to the counter to pay, and left.

Micky felt none the wiser for having seen Robin.

"And?" Amber was already sitting next to her again.

Micky just shrugged. "I really don't know. She said to call her and something about being friends with benefits."

"Hm." Amber got that overly empathic expression on her face she so often wore. "What do *you* want, Micky?"

"I honestly have no fucking clue." Micky needed time to think. She could do with not having a job right then, with having all the time in the world to mull this over. And to finally come to the one conclusion that she hadn't allowed herself to reach yet: was she a lesbian or not?

"Chances are you'll be seeing her again tomorrow. What are you going to say to her?"

"How does that even work?" Micky failed to reply to Amber's question directly. "Being friends with benefits? You and I are best friends, Amber. Doesn't that give us loads of benefits already?"

"You do have the benefit of all my free advice." Amber shot her a silly smile.

"Yes, that's true. I do remember you telling me to take this job and to reply with a resounding yes if a hot female customer were to flirt with me. So many benefits." Micky was getting giddy with fatigue and a strange kind of weariness.

"All included in my friendship," Amber said.

"I'd better get back to it. I won't be at yoga this

afternoon. I need a nap before the kids come home." Micky inhaled deeply. When she walked to the counter, it was as though she could feel a tingle in all the places where Robin had touched her the night before.

CHAPTER NINE

"She didn't come in for the rest of the week," Micky said. She and Amber had only been at Kristin and Sheryl's well-appointed apartment for ten minutes before the conversation had turned to Robin.

Josephine, with her big mouth, had told Kristin at the change of shift on Thursday. "Micky's a bit upset because her girlfriend hasn't come in today," she'd said.

The worst part of it was that it was true. Micky was genuinely thrown by Robin's absence. What was she meant to do now? Text Robin like she had said? And what would she say? *I'm ready for some more of the benefits that come with our flimsy friendship*? The more Micky had thought about it, the more ridiculous it sounded. Maybe she wasn't ready for a big romance, but well, maybe she was? Because what else was she going to do? Play the field?

"I'm sure she'll come by tomorrow," Kristin had said. But Robin hadn't shown her face again. Micky had lingered after her shift, munching on a croissant at a table near the door, in case Robin's work schedule had changed and she came in later.

Now it was Saturday evening, and they all sat gathered around Kristin and Sheryl's table sipping excellent wine, and Micky didn't know what to do. She didn't want this dinner at her boss's to be all about this, but truth be told, it was pretty much all Micky had been thinking about. Whether she wanted it to be or not, this was a huge deal for her.

"Why don't you text her now?" Amber offered. "So we'll all be here when she replies. You won't be alone."

Micky wanted to sink through the floor with embarrassment. But Kristin had been the one to ask her about it, and now here she sat, discussing Robin again.

"What would I say?" Micky looked up, straight into Sheryl's face. Micky hadn't spent a lot of time with Sheryl, and Kristin's wife was still a bit of an enigma to her. They'd only exchanged pleasantries at The Pink Bean, but not much else. What must this woman think of her? This accomplished professor who sat there with one leg slung over the other, sipping her wine as though she knew all about wines and their grapes of origin.

Sheryl shot Micky an encouraging smile. "Why don't you simply say hello," she said.

"Look, ladies, I don't want tonight to be all about me and this…" Micky had trouble qualifiying it. What was this anyway?

"Kristin and I have been together for a long time. Please, do us the favor of being able to live vicariously through you for a bit." Sheryl took a sip of wine. "This is exciting."

"Micky is quite new to this," Amber said.

"Quite?" Micky repeated. "Until a year ago, I was married to a man."

"All the more reason to enjoy this delicious time of discovery." Sheryl's voice was matter-of-fact.

Micky had had ample sleep since her night with Robin. Her life had returned to normal, almost as though Micky hadn't, for the very first time, touched another woman like that. In a way, it was comforting to be able to slip into the routine of everyday life. To wear that coat of normalcy. But it *had* happened, and when Robin failed to show at her regular time at The Pink Bean twice, Micky had to draw the obvious conclusion. Robin had probably met another friend with benefits—because how many of those could one person realistically have?

"I like her," Micky admitted. She might as well. It was

not often that she found herself in the company of lesbians who understood what she was going through. "But we're very incompatible. So why even bother?"

"Focus on the first thing you said," Kristin said. "You like her."

"I'm forty-four years old. I can't go texting a woman I have a crush on like that. It feels so... incredibly immature."

"That's not how I see it," Sheryl said. "You're doing the very brave thing of coming out later in life. That's not easy. You have a lot to take into consideration, but in the end, you're doing it for yourself, for your happiness. If you think Robin can bring you some happiness, why not try?"

"Moreover, you haven't experienced your lesbian puberty," Kristin added. "This is perfectly normal behavior for someone in your situation."

"Text her," Amber urged. "What's the worst that can happen?"

"She doesn't reply and then comes into the coffee shop on Monday and pretends we never even knew each other," Micky was quick to say.

Kristin shook her head. "Worst case scenario: we lose a customer."

"I've only been working at The Pink Bean for two weeks, and I would have already lost you a customer."

"The Pink Bean has plenty of other customers," Sheryl said.

"So you're all saying I should text her?" Micky took a big gulp of wine.

"Yes" came the unified reply.

Micky felt a twinge of guilt when she reached into her purse for her phone. She was always admonishing her children when they used their phones in social situations— usually the dinner table. She liked to believe she had raised them better than that. But the pull of a smartphone—the dozen dopamine shots it delivered to the brain with every new notification that pinged and every new message that arrived—was irresistible to a teenager. Now to Micky as well.

"I'll just say 'Hey, how are you?'" Micky said, then did so. "There. Done." She put her phone on the table. "Now, please, let's talk about something else. The way we've been going on about my one-night stand, you'd think we were all still in college instead of being mature adults." Micky raised her glass. "Thank you so much for inviting us over."

✳ ✳ ✳

Kristin, who appeared to be a domestic goddess as well as a pristine-looking, savvy businesswoman—Micky dreaded to think how much she paled in comparison to so much suave and expertise at life—had already served the mains of scrumptious home-made ravioli with wild mushrooms, and Micky still hadn't received a text back.

As the night progressed and she'd poured more wine into her system, she'd adopted more of an oh-well attitude. At least her first time with a woman had been spectacular. At least she knew she wanted more. Robin wasn't right for her anyway. Maybe now that she was more open to the idea of dating women, she should start the internet dating Amber was so against. Amber didn't need to know.

"So it was an amicable divorce?" Micky heard Sheryl ask. She'd zoned out of the conversation for a second. The professor sure liked to ask the pertinent questions.

"As amicable as a divorce can be," Micky said. "But Darren and I didn't want to create a hostile environment for the kids." Though, for a while, despite their best intentions, of course they had. Telling your kids that their home is being ripped apart will always be hostile.

"And the reason for the divorce was?" The more Sheryl drank of that exquisite wine she served, the more probing her questions became.

"Not what you might think." Micky gave a nervous chuckle. "Our marriage just didn't work anymore. It hadn't for a while. The thought of having to stay with Darren for the rest of my life in what, perhaps for most people, looked like a perfectly acceptable union, depressed the hell out of me. When I first realized we were more like best friends than anything else, I thought, well, that works for me. Turned out it didn't. We grew more distant. Darren works very long hours. I was always at home. The kids grew up. Then I woke up one day and had a long hard look at my life and wondered why the hell I was throwing it away."

"Good for you." Sheryl raised her glass.

"It was the hardest thing I've ever done." Micky remembered the agony of waking up every morning and having to drag herself through another dreadful day of everything being exactly the same—and the complete opposite of how she wanted it to be.

"But in the end, one of the best," Amber said.

Micky looked at her best friend. "Of course, Amber here, with all her psychic gifts, had seen it coming from miles away."

"I guess I got a first hint of how unhappy you were when you started talking about exactly how hot Claire Underwood is in *House of Cards*." Amber turned to Kristin and Sheryl. "The monologues I've sat through on the subject."

"I wasn't that bad," Micky said in her defense. "Besides, any creature with a pulse thinks Claire Underwood is the hottest woman to have ever graced the small screen. It's pretty universal."

"While there's definitely some truth in that," Sheryl said, "it must have given you an inkling of how you really felt about women?"

"Yes, when did you know?" Kristin asked.

Wow. All inhibitions were cast aside now. This was the sort of subject Micky never addressed, apart from a halfhearted conversation with Amber. But Amber always knew when to stop—probably because she wasn't a big consumer of alcohol like the other people at this table.

"Really know? Not that long ago. But I have to admit I

was in denial for a very long time. I was also happily married for almost two decades. It just, I don't know, never really occurred to me." Micky glanced at Amber. "Even though, all the while, my very best friend was a lesbian."

"Talk about being in denial," Amber said. "Denial is probably not even the correct word to describe how deep you had buried your true desires."

"Better late than never," Sheryl said. "I applaud your courage. I dread to think how many women in your position don't take any steps and just continue with their passionless lives."

"What about you guys? How long have you been together?" Micky felt like talking about something other than herself.

"We'll be celebrating our twenty years together next year," Kristin said, placing a hand on Sheryl's shoulder. "Gush about me all you want, honey." She pecked Sheryl on the cheek. "I'm going to get dessert ready."

"Do you need a hand with that?" Amber asked. She wasn't nearly as intoxicated as Micky was. She didn't wait for Kristin's reply, and they both disappeared into the kitchen together.

"Twenty years," Micky repeated. "I'm so in awe of that." They must have gotten together around the same time she and Darren had met—a lifetime ago.

"As corny as it sounds, I guess we're soul mates. Kristin has been the one and only for me for twenty years now, and I wouldn't want it any other way."

That did sound corny, but also very beautiful.

"Let me tell you something, Micky." Sheryl leaned over the table. She was obviously the biggest drinker of the pair. "It's important to surround yourself with like-minded people. It really is. Of course, times are different now. Everything is much more open and accepted, but if I hadn't had the support network I had when I was younger, I wouldn't be sitting here with my partner of twenty years today. You were lucky to have Amber, and now you have us as well, okay?"

"Okay," Micky said. She wasn't that tipsy to know that sometimes, under the influence, some people were prone to make big declarations. Or maybe this was just the kind of person Sheryl was. Sitting here in her and Kristin's home, Amber by her side, Micky felt as though she had started a new chapter in her life. "At least I'm out at work," she joked.

"No news from Robin yet, huh?" Sheryl sank back into her chair.

"It's okay. Not having to sit at home and obsess about it on my own while my children are in their rooms doing God knows what really helps."

Amber and Kristin emerged from the kitchen, each carrying a plate.

"Apple crumble for dessert," Kristin said. "I hope there's some room left in your bellies."

Micky might not have the tiniest bit of appetite left after the scrumptious meal Kristin had already served, but what she had plenty of space for in her heart and in her life, were new friends like these.

CHAPTER TEN

The first thing Micky did when she woke up on Sunday morning, was reach for her phone. When she'd arrived home late the night before, she'd drunkenly taken it into the bedroom with her. She still hadn't received a text back from Robin, which, despite having had a wonderful evening last night, didn't sit right with her. Why the silence? If Robin wanted to be friends—be it with benefits or not—shouldn't she at least have the courtesy to text back?

Micky felt like one of her teenagers when she checked her phone for messages like this in bed. Nine times out of ten, when she opened Olivia's bedroom door—after knocking first, of course—she'd find her daughter in the position she was now lying in herself, painfully uncomfortable. Christopher was more glued to his laptop screen than to his phone, playing the online versions of the video games she and Darren had always refused to buy for him.

On her phone, Micky found a message from Amber, sent two hours ago. Of course, Amber had been up since the crack of dawn. She'd probably already meditated for an hour and repotted some plants. If anyone was the polar opposite of Micky, it was her best friend. And they'd managed to be friends for almost forty years.

What a great night last night. They're definitely keepers! See you tonight, Amber's message read. Micky's best friend couldn't help it. She even sounded upbeat in her text messages, even the ones sent frightfully early on a Sunday morning. The message also reminded Micky that she, the kids, and Amber were having dinner at her mother's that night. Micky and Amber always joked that they were more like sisters than friends, but after Amber's parents had both passed away in quick succession more than fourteen years ago—sparking Amber's zest to adopt an ultra-healthy lifestyle—Micky's mother had, in fact, started treating Amber as one of her own.

Next, Micky went on Facebook. The only reason she was even on that particular social network—or any other one—was to see what her children were up to. It had caused a bit of a ruckus at the breakfast table one day when Micky had created her profile and sent Olivia a friend request.

"But you're my mom," her daughter had said, as though it was the most self-explanatory sentence in the world.

"Exactly," Micky had replied. "We know each other. I can even mark you as family."

Olivia, only eleven at the time, had rolled her eyes, and said, "Just don't go posting embarrassing things on my wall."

"She just wants to check up on us," Christopher had said, hitting the nail on the head exactly.

"And what if I do?" Micky's parenting style wasn't one of subtleness and discretion.

Neither Olivia, nor Christopher had posted something since the last time she checked. They'd probably moved on to the next big thing. Micky had heard Olivia mention something like Snapchat the other day—"All the celebs are on there these days."—with great excitement in her voice.

Darren, on the other hand, had been tagged by one of his Facebook-crazy mates at a pub in the CBD. Micky couldn't help it, but her heart always skipped a beat when Darren was mentioned, on Facebook or elsewhere. She was gripped by an irrational fear that he'd soon replace Micky.

Despite a slightly protruding middle-age waistline, he was a good-looking single man with a nice chunk of change in the bank. Off the top of her head, Micky could easily think of plenty of women who would find that irresistible. Of course, Darren shared equal custody of the kids with her, which might make him seem a little less attractive to prospective love interests. Having two teenagers in the house half the time isn't the biggest love drug—Micky could testify to that.

But on weekends when the kids were with her, Micky was always extra wary when she checked Facebook and saw Darren's name appear. He might have met someone at that pub he was at last night. Who knew? Was her ex-husband waking up alone this morning? They didn't have the kind of post-divorce relationship where Micky could just ask him. They got along, but the wound of the separation was still too raw for them to have already crossed over into friendship.

While Micky was pondering Darren's love life, her phone beeped, causing her heart to fling itself against her rib cage.

It was from Robin.

Had to go out of town unexpectedly for a few days. Back this afternoon. Wanna meet up tonight?

Micky sat up a bit straighter. Ouch. Her head hurt more than anticipated when she did. This was good. Robin hadn't been avoiding her. And she wanted to meet up tonight. That was out of the question, of course. Micky pondered what to do. Should she reply immediately or wait at least an hour? To hell with it. She was replying now. She wanted to have a real conversation with Robin, one that would take away that nagging feeling in her gut of not knowing what to do and how to behave in this new-to-her situation.

Can't tonight. Kids are here. Tomorrow evening? She texted back.

Micky figured she could sneak out for a quick drink tomorrow. Olivia always went swimming on Monday evening, and Christopher would barely notice she was gone.

OK. I'll see you at The Pink Bean in the morning. We can set it up then.

Micky's headache suddenly didn't seem so bad anymore. She jumped out of bed and into the shower.

★ ★ ★

With her kids in the backseat of the car, Micky couldn't tell Amber about her text message exchange with Robin. She'd tried to steal her away from the kids when she'd arrived, but both Olivia and Christopher seemed to always perk up around their Aunt Amber. It must be her positive energy. Something Amber had tried to school Micky in many a time, but Micky must have a different kind of spirit because no matter what Amber said or did, it never stuck. Still, it was always nice to be around her. She always glowed with good health and vibes. She was also godmother to both of Micky's children.

When Christopher was born, Micky hadn't even had to think about it. There was no competition. Micky didn't have any brothers or sisters and Amber was her best friend and had been since they were six. Darren knew the score and didn't object, knowing how important it was to Micky to give Amber a role like that in their firstborn's life, despite the fact that his sister Daisy was also in serious contention for the part.

When Olivia was born, though, Darren had assumed godmother-hood would automatically go to his sister, but Amber had just lost her father, to whom she was very close, a mere sixteen months after her mother had passed, and Micky had so desperately wanted to give her best friend the gift of life in some form. Amber was not the kind to take being a child's godmother lightly. She was full-on, and she doted on Christopher. Micky had also assumed that Amber wouldn't have any children of her own any time soon.

Moreover, and this was the most important aspect of it for Micky, if, God forbid, anything were to happen to her and Darren, she wanted Amber to take care of her children. Sure, Daisy was Darren's sister, but she had children of her own—a third on the way at the time—and they simply weren't as close. Not even Darren was as close to his own sister as Micky was to Amber. He sure saw a great deal more of Amber than he did of Daisy. Amber fitted into their lives better. And she needed it so badly at that time.

There had been some discussions, full-blown rows even, about who would become Olivia's godmother, until Darren had given in. He knew how important it was to Micky, and in the end, he was that kind of guy. They were at the height of their happiness together—Micky was carrying his second child. Thus, Amber had become godmother to both Olivia and Christopher. Micky had certainly never regretted her decision—and she gratefully remembered Darren's willingness to acquiesce.

Micky was sure that her children, especially Olivia, told Amber things they would never tell her. Despite their mother's friendship with Amber, they knew their aunt Amber would never tell on them. The fact that she was that kind of person just radiated off of her. They were both also fully aware of Amber's sexual preference and had seen a few of Amber's longer-term partners come and go. Having grown up with it, to Olivia and Christopher, it just didn't seem to be a big deal. Micky was convinced, however, that when they found out their mother shared the same inclination as their beloved godmother, it *would* be an issue. How could it not be?

"How's your girlfriend, Chris?" Amber teased.

"As if he has a girlfriend," Olivia said with the sort of disdain in her voice only a teenager could muster. "He's in love with a character in *League of Legends* more like."

Micky did sometimes worry about the amount of time her eldest spent in his room. But Christopher gave her much less lip than Olivia and he was, by far, the most easygoing of the two, so she refused to give him a hard time about it.

"Shut up, Liv. You don't know anything," Chris said.

Amber didn't engage them in conversation any more,

and they went on bickering in the backseat while Micky drove them to her mother's house in Mosman—not far from where she, Darren, and the kids used to live. The fact that both Micky and Darren had moved away from the leafy suburb had broken her mother's heart a little, Micky was sure of that. But should she really have stayed in the same neighborhood she'd lived in all of her life just for her mother's sake? Micky had definitely contemplated it, but the kids were growing up so fast and spending time with their granny Gina wasn't so high on their to-do list anymore. A fact Micky's mother was well aware of and had resigned herself to in the end.

When they arrived, Micky gave her mother an extra tight hug because she was feeling guilty about a number of things. Not only about moving her grandchildren away to the city but also about the fact that, since she'd last seen her mother, Micky had slept with another woman.

✶ ✶ ✶

Micky's mother was one of the most understanding parents there were, Micky was sure of that. She had never had unreasonable expectations of her only child and had done everything in her power to make Micky thrive. She'd even been understanding about the divorce—"When it's over, it's over."—though Micky hadn't told her the full truth about it.

Would she ever have to come out to her mother?

Micky shook off the thought and helped her in the kitchen while Amber took Olivia and Christopher's phones away and put them in the huge handbag she always carried around.

"Come on. We're going into the garden," she said, receiving nothing but loud moans from her godchildren. "Get some fresh air."

"Amber will have them in crow pose in no time," Micky joked, earning a quizzical look from her mother.

"How are you, darling?" Micky's mom always made a point of asking as soon as they were alone. As though the kids couldn't handle the possible answer to that question.

"I'm well." There was the guilt again. Just like her children had done, Micky's mother had witnessed Amber's coming out from up close. There had been the usual comments, especially when Micky's father had still been alive, of "I would never have guessed, a pretty girl like that" and "How will she ever find happiness being like that in a world like ours?"

Even though Micky had a good rapport with her only surviving parent, she and her mother didn't have the kind of relationship in which they shared everything. Gina had remained single after her husband had passed, and Micky never questioned her about that. Micky did wonder if her mother would start questioning her once she believed the time was right—but when would that be? One year after her divorce from Darren had been finalized perhaps? Right about now.

"I've heard something... I was having lunch at the beach club the other day, and I overheard two women I don't even know talking. It took me a while to realize it was Darren they were discussing. Apparently he's been seeing one of the women's daughter. Someone called Lisa. They described him as a right catch. Did you know?"

That was really forward of Gina. Usually she'd ease into a conversation like this, but it must have been nagging at her, the way she was blurting it out now. And hell no, Micky didn't know. The last time she'd spoken to Darren, it was to discuss Olivia's latest dentist appointment and how unhappy she was that she needed braces. They only talked when they had to and when it involved the children, not having much else to say to each other at this stage.

"No." It was, however, not jealousy Micky felt coursing through her. On the contrary. Despite having dreaded this moment, she could pretty easily—and unexpectedly—conceive of being happy for Darren, though, of course, bringing another person into the kids' lives would have to be discussed at length. That feeling in her gut, Micky recognized, was the sense that she had failed. That her marriage had failed. That, apart from her two beautiful children, Micky didn't have that much to show for in life. In fact, all she had was a vague text from another woman on her phone promising a conversation Micky didn't know how to have. That, and the memory of, quite surely, a night of the very best sex of her life. "I'm sure he'll fill me in when and if it gets serious," Micky said.

"I couldn't keep that from you, love. And I wanted to tell you in person, not over the phone."

Micky just nodded. "Thanks for telling me."

Then the kids burst back in, and the moment of impromptu information sharing was over.

Micky could hardly blame Darren for moving on. After all, she'd been trying to do the exact same thing.

CHAPTER ELEVEN

That morning, Robin had come into The Pink Bean, requesting her usual drink, at an uncharacteristically busy time. Micky had barely had time to talk to her, even though Robin patiently waited, take-out coffee cup in hand. In between serving customers, they managed to set up a time to talk tonight, at the same bar they'd met at last Tuesday evening.

As soon as Olivia left the house, bag with swimsuit and goggles in hand, her swimming buddy April waiting outside, Micky gently rapped on Christopher's bedroom door. Of course, he didn't hear, not even when she intensified the knocking, so she ended up opening up his bedroom door without waiting for a reply—she could have waited for days!

"What?" Christopher said, barely looking up from his screen.

"Did you finish your homework?" Micky always thought she had to ask, even though Christopher got good grades.

"I'm finishing it now."

"I'm going out for a walk. I won't be long."

Then, Christopher looked away from his screen, scanning her face. Micky never went for random walks, but there was a first time for everything.

"I've decided to adopt a healthier lifestyle," she said. "Aunt Amber constantly being on my case about it must be having an effect." Micky felt like a fool for lying to her son like that. She could have just said she was meeting a friend for a drink. It could be perfectly innocent—except, it wasn't.

"Okay." With that, Christopher focused his attention back on whatever fascinating thing he was doing on his laptop.

More guilt settled in the pit of her stomach as Micky checked her reflection in the hallway mirror and went to meet Robin.

✳ ✳ ✳

Just like last time, Robin was already there, an open bottle of wine on the table in front of her.

"I got you a glass already," Robin said, instead of hello.

"Thanks." Micky slid onto the high stool, feeling awkward for not having exchanged a peck on the cheek or greeting Robin the way she would greet any other human being. All she could think of, after having been in Robin's vicinity for mere seconds, was how she wanted to feel her hands all over her body again. How could they have shared such intimacy, and sit here like almost-strangers now?

Robin poured Micky a generous helping of wine, of which Micky took a quick, large gulp.

When Micky set her glass down and looked back up, Robin was smiling broadly at her. "Nervous?" she asked.

"Yeah, I can't stay long. Liv's out swimming, but she knows she needs to be home by eight thirty, and Chris thinks I'm out for a walk."

"Relax." Robin's smile persisted.

"I'm sorry. I just feel like I'm… I don't know. Committing adultery or something." What was she saying? Micky wasn't there to discuss the ever-growing sensation of guilt that had lodged itself deep inside of her. She was there to discuss how to become Robin's *friend with benefits*. Because, oh, she wanted those benefits.

"Take another sip. It'll make you feel better." Robin slid Micky's glass a little closer in her direction. "Not that I'm pushing you toward alcoholism or anything."

Micky drank, then drank some more. Christopher would never believe she'd gone for a walk when he smelled the wine on her breath. She'd have to brush her teeth as soon as she got home.

"Okay. I'm ready now," Micky said, though she was nowhere near ready and she didn't even know what to be ready for.

"Do you want to get together this weekend?" Robin asked. "I've only been in Sydney for a couple of months. I could do with a friend showing me around."

Micky's brain was rapidly—and madly—trying to interpret what Robin had just said. Did she mean anything by it? Would they end up at Robin's place again? Would they be able to wake up together on a peaceful Sunday morning?

"The kids are at their dad's, so yes. I would love that."

"Can you believe I haven't been to the beach yet? The first few months in a new city are always crazy. Finding a place, making it feel a bit homely, trying to meet people, all squeezed in between getting acquainted with a new workplace and new colleagues."

"That must be tough, moving from one city to another like that."

"It's what I chose, but mind you, after Singapore and Hong Kong, coming to Sydney is a walk in the park, really. I shouldn't complain."

"I'll take you to the beach. We might even get lucky with the weather."

"Look, Micky." Robin's facial expression turned serious. "I find it very important to not lead you on. Though we discussed it last time, I feel I should repeat that I'm not really in the market for anything too serious. It's not really what I do. I'm only going to be here until the end of the year, anyway. I just want to put that out there."

"All right," Micky heard herself say, while pangs of anguish burrowed their way through her flesh. "I'm not exactly relationship material either." She managed a weak chuckle.

"I would like for us to be friends. Very much so."

"Yeah, that would be nice."

"Have you thought about what I said the other day?" Robin had lowered her voice. "About being friends *with* benefits?"

"Er, yes, I have." Micky hadn't thought of much else. "I guess we could give that a try."

"I don't want you to do anything that makes you feel uncomfortable." Robin started taking faster and faster swigs from her wine—quickly emptying it like she did with her coffee at The Pink Bean.

"It doesn't make me uncomfortable," Micky mumbled. "I basically don't have much of a clue of what I'm doing."

"I really enjoyed our time together last week." Robin painted on that smile again. "*Really.*"

"Me too." Micky sipped more wine, hoping to hide the blush that she felt creeping up her neck. "I, er, am just curious. Are you…" If Micky ever had any defined plan of how her entrée into lesbian life would go, having a conversation like this was never part of it.

"Yes?" Robin leaned over the table, creating more intimacy between them.

"Are you friends with benefits with other women as well?" There, she'd said it. Micky could imagine getting to know Robin better and looking forward to spending more time with her in the bedroom, but drawing a firm line at friendship. What she couldn't fathom was Robin courting other women and bringing them to her apartment and rocking their world the way she had done with Micky. That just felt totally off—wrong even.

"Not at the moment."

"I'm going to be very honest here. I was married for eighteen years, and that is all I know. Any new relationship forms out there, I'm not very aware of. You're going to have to spell this out for me without being coy, because I do feel like I have a right to know."

"I'm not in the habit of seeing multiple women at the

same time, nor am I in the habit of attaching myself to one person too closely. I can't afford to do that." Robin refilled both their glasses. "Before I moved here, I lived in Hong Kong for two years. I had one sort-of relationship, but we kept it casual because we both knew I would be leaving."

"Wasn't that hard to do?"

"Not if you know from the start and you act accordingly. Michelle and I never went on romantic breaks to Thai islands together like other couples did, for instance, because we weren't a couple."

"You were friends with benefits."

Robin nodded. "That doesn't mean I didn't have feelings for her. We're still close. I talk to her every week. She'll come visit me in a couple of months. But we're not together, because we never were."

This caught Micky's attention more than anything else Robin had said. "So, when this Michelle comes over, will she be staying with you?"

"Yes, of course. She'll be sleeping on the couch, though." Robin scrunched her lips together. "The only way to know if you're really cut out for this, is to try, Micky. I promise to take your feelings into consideration as much as I can and to always be completely honest with you. I will never deceive you and will always be up-front about everything. That's how I live."

Then the alarm on Micky's phone buzzed. She'd set it just before she left the house so she could return home on time without rousing suspicion. "I have to go."

Robin nodded. "I'll see you at The Pink Bean this week, and if for some reason I don't, I'll call you. Is that okay?"

"Yes. That would be fine." Micky stared into Robin's eyes a bit longer than she would into a friend's without benefits. Then, she couldn't stop herself. She slid off the stool and kissed Robin on the cheek. She had to feel her skin against her own, even for the briefest of moments. "See you," she said, and turned on her heel.

CHAPTER TWELVE

Because of what her mother had told her on Sunday, Micky wasn't overly surprised when Darren called later that week, asking if she could meet him for lunch at a restaurant near his office on Friday.

"My shift ends at twelve," Micky said. "I can be there by one thirty." She wasn't going to meet Darren at one of the upscale restaurants he frequented for lunch straight after serving coffee for five and a half hours. She needed to go home and shower first. And there would be traffic to contend with. Perhaps she should try to get Darren to come to her and finally put a stop to how she had always accommodated him, because, after all, he was the one who brought home the bacon.

He still did. Micky's lawyer had negotiated generous alimony payments for her, allowing her to afford the rent on her small but expensive new house in Darlinghurst. Micky didn't feel guilty about it because she knew he could easily afford it and because, when she really started thinking about it, she had worked *for* Darren for eighteen years. She had given birth to their children, raised them in his frequent absence, and dealt with everything that comes with running a household on her own. All Darren ever had to worry about was going to work and making money. She wondered how he was coping now during the weeks he had the kids. Of course, they were so independent now, and Darren paid someone to cook them healthy dinners.

"Oh yeah, Liv told me you're working at a coffeehouse now," he said, with no audible judgment in his tone.

Micky could only conclude that Darren was feeling some kind of negative emotion about having to tell her about Lisa, otherwise he would surely have made a snide remark or, at the very least, inquired about whether she needed more money.

"One thirty is fine," Darren said. "See you then."

Now Micky was negotiating traffic, which was always such a pain in the ass in this direction, no matter the time of day. But she tried to keep an optimistic attitude, and it gave her some time to think. She imagined having to have the conversation that Darren wanted to have with her, having to tell him there was someone new in her life and it being a woman.

In the very beginning of their courtship, Micky had told Darren about Janet, the girl she had had a crush on in her last year of high school. But nothing had ever happened between Micky and Janet, and in the end, there hadn't been that much to tell.

When Micky first breached the topic of separation, almost three years ago, one of Darren's first questions had been whether there was someone else, but it wouldn't even have occurred to him that, if there had been, it would most likely have been a woman. Or not. Micky was still buried so deep in the closet then. She didn't even know what she wanted. All she knew was that she couldn't be married to Darren anymore. That her life needed to change drastically and that the time had come for Micky Ferro to put herself first after giving the best years of her life—gladly and willingly—to her family.

What had Sheryl said last Saturday? That it took a lot of courage to do what Micky had done. To uproot her life the way she had. But for Micky, courage wasn't what had made her take the first step away from Darren. It was pure necessity.

In the beginning, she'd had to put all her energy into making Darren understand that it wasn't about him. It wasn't. Darren Steele was a perfectly good man. He worked too hard, spent too much time away from home and his children, and when he was home, his mind was often elsewhere. But he was never aggressive in any way; he didn't drink too much; he didn't have time to even think about other women. But that was also what he had become to Micky. Acceptable. When she looked at him, she no longer found him dashing, sexy, or even particularly relevant apart from being the father of her children. They didn't sleep in separate bedrooms, but they might as well have.

After fifteen years of marriage, it felt more as though they were simply going through the motions of how life should be, and Micky was so sick of it. And then there was that other thing.

After Janet, Micky had never had a crush like that on another woman again. Maybe because she didn't allow herself to, or maybe because she was afraid.

Micky honked the horn at a taxi cutting her off. She was about to give him the finger as well but then thought better of it. Driving around with children in the backseat had taught her to control most of her impulsive reactions.

Her children. Micky had dedicated her life to her children. Now it was her turn.

Micky finally reached the underground parking lot. Back in the day, before she had been pregnant with Christopher, Micky often drove up to Sydney's Central Business District to meet Darren for lunch. She could easily park in the streets back then. So much had changed since then.

✷ ✷ ✷

Because Micky picked the kids up from school after their week with Darren, she didn't see him very often. They mostly spoke on the phone, and only when they had to.

She would never forget that deeply hurt look on Darren's face when she'd first told him she wanted to separate. He looked as though she'd just told him someone had kidnapped Olivia. First there was shock and disbelief, then a flash of rage. But Darren was Darren, and he quickly composed himself, started to ask her questions so he could analyze the situation with his mathematical brain. "What have I done wrong?" "Which steps can we take to fix this?" "Is there someone else?"

It had cost so much energy to convince Darren that, all things considered, Micky wanting a divorce had little to do with him—in as far as that was possible. They were in the marriage together, of course, had built this life together.

"You look good, Micky," Darren said now. Was that a touch of nostalgia coating his voice? He got up from the table where he'd already been sitting, glued to his phone screen when Micky walked in—Christopher and Olivia certainly didn't get that tendency from a stranger.

"So do you." It wasn't even a lie. Darren had lost some weight around his waist. Micky guessed his new girlfriend might have something to do with that. Perhaps she got him to do what Micky never could: join a gym. "For your health," Micky would say. "You need to burn off the stress somehow." But Micky was hardly a good example herself. Granted, she was a regular at Amber's yoga classes, but as far as Darren was concerned, yoga wasn't exercise.

"How are the kids?" she asked as soon as she sat down. It was an automatic question she always asked Darren when they were with him. After the divorce, not having her kids live under her roof had been the biggest adjustment for Micky. Even if they spent a lot of their time in their rooms, just having them present in the house was enough for her. Not having them there for a week at a time was pure torture in the beginning. That was another reason Micky couldn't stay in the house in Mosman. If she'd stayed there, too much would have remained the same.

"Olivia wants to go to a sleepover at April's on Saturday. I'm going to call Chuck and see what's what. I have a sneaking suspicion Allison is watching her younger sister while their parents are out of town."

It was odd to hear Darren talk about things like that. Before the divorce, Micky would have always been the one to inform him about matters like these, but now he had to be involved in his children's lives a lot more.

"Not to worry, I won't let her stay with the Hartmanns unsupervised." He held up a bottle of Perrier. "Water?" Darren would never drink alcohol if he had to go back to the office after lunch.

Micky nodded.

"How's the job panning out?" he asked while pouring her a glass.

"It keeps me busy." Micky drank from the water and glanced at Darren over the rim of her glass to gauge his reaction.

"I figured you weren't doing it for the money."

"Waitresses get a decent wage in Australia, so it's nothing to sneeze at." Of course, Micky wasn't working at The Pink Bean for the money.

"Olivia did have something to say about it being The Pink Bean," Darren said, taking Micky by surprise. "Is there anything you need to tell me, Micks?" Darren had a huge grin on his face.

Micky's heart was beating furiously. For a split second, she thought her ex-husband had her all figured out. Then she realized he was just joking. Just like Micky for the longest of time, he didn't have a clue.

"You'll be the first to know," she said in a tone that didn't bear contesting.

A waiter brought over menus, and Micky buried her nose in hers, though she seemed to have lost her appetite.

After placing their order and talking about Olivia's braces and a too-boisterous classmate Christopher seemed to be spending most of his time with at school, Darren cleared his throat. "There's something you should know, Micky. I've met someone." Darren never was one to beat about the bush.

Micky nodded thoughtfully.

"Her name is Lisa. I met her at The Brew Dog at Friday night happy hour. We've been seeing each other for a few weeks now, and I would like to introduce her to the kids. It's a little difficult not to, and they're clever things. They'll figure it out soon enough, if they haven't already."

"If they have, they haven't spoken to me about it," Micky said, then wondered if she should congratulate her ex-husband on getting it on with someone new. "Good for you, Darren. I'm happy you met someone."

"She works in finance, like me. For the competition, though, so I'm not sure how that will work out." He gave an awkward chuckle—Darren Steele was not an awkward-chuckle kind of man.

"Which bank?" Micky's heart started thudding again.

"Goodwin Stark." Darren didn't think to ask why Micky was inquiring. Why would he?

Micky wished she had a glass of wine at her disposal. Her ex-husband's new girlfriend was a colleague of the woman she had slept with. Fuck.

"I was planning on filling in the kids this weekend. Possibly tonight so I have the rest of the weekend with them in case they have questions. Then I could have Lisa over on Sunday so they can get to know her." He drummed his fingertips on the tabletop. "Do you want to meet her?"

Micky didn't know what the protocol was for this sort of thing. This woman would be in her children's lives so she supposed she should at least get to know her a little. "In time. I trust your judgment." Micky could not face sitting opposite Lisa any time soon, however. She would need some time to process all the information.

"I chose you, after all." Darren really was full of jokes today. Maybe it was the effect of being in love again.

Micky quirked up her eyebrows, then said, "It's okay. As I said, I trust you to have their best interests at heart."

Darren worked too much, but he had always been a good father. If anything, it was Micky who was feeling like a bad mother because of her own romantic interests. "I'll meet her in due course." Micky proceeded to tell Darren what her mother had told her.

"If it has reached the Mosman Beach Club, it'll be all over Sydney in no time," Darren said.

CHAPTER THIRTEEN

When she lived in Mosman, Micky had gone to the beach often—at least twice a week. She preferred to go in winter, when she could be alone and just have an hour to herself, thinking of nothing and just watching the tide roll in.

The trip to the beach she was to undertake that day would be very different from those back in the day, when she was still a married woman.

She was going to the beach with Robin.

It made her feel so giddy, Micky actually mocked herself when she passed a mirror and caught her reflection. "You silly twat," she said to herself, then she would grin uncontrollably.

If it were up to Micky, they would skip this trip to the beach entirely and just go back to Robin's flat. Every evening since that night, before she went to sleep, Micky allowed herself the delicious luxury of reliving the memory. The best part, for her, had been when Robin had said, "Not bad for a beginner." Not the words as such, but the way she had said them. Her voice full of satisfaction, her pupils dilated, her smile so soft and convincing.

Micky was still a beginner, but the first-time nerves were out of the way now. All she wanted was to do it again, and again.

She packed her bikini, a towel, sunscreen, and her most glamorous pair of sunglasses into a bag, and went to pick up Robin. It felt so strange to drive her car through the few streets it took to get to Robin's flat and pick up *another woman*. It was a brand new experience for Micky. It was exhilarating.

Robin was waiting for her outside her building and, as soon as she got into the car, handed Micky a paper cup of coffee from The Pink Bean.

"I had to bribe the barista to find out what you liked," she said, a big smile on her face.

"It's not a wet capp, is it?" Micky smiled back.

"You should have seen your face when I placed that order. I think I decided to ask you out there and then."

Micky shook her head. "Oh, please."

"Hi, Micky." Robin slanted in her direction and placed a kiss on her cheek.

Micky inhaled Robin's scent and, for an instant, contemplated asking if they could skip the beach and go straight up to her flat. They could even go back to her house. It was all empty and inviting and ready for all the sex Micky wanted to have. Oh my. She was feeling rather frisky today.

Instead, she took a sip from the coffee and placed the cup in the holder. "All set?"

"You bet." Robin's voice was dripping with excitement. "The last beach I was at was an overly busy one in Hong Kong, chock-full of unruly mainland China tourists, and the water wasn't exactly crystal clear. I've been googling pictures of Bondi beach, and it looks so stunning."

Micky could hardly take Robin to Balmoral, the beach she knew so well in Mosman. They were bound to run into someone familiar there. Bondi was much bigger, more anonymous, and very gay friendly. They could easily disappear into the crowd—just be two friends enjoying the sun, sand, and surf. There was another s-word Micky kept thinking about. She should really get a grip. What was she? Twenty-four instead of forty-four?

"Thank you so much for taking me," Robin said in between sipping from her coffee.

It was at the same time exciting and excruciating to sit

in a car with her. She was so close, when Micky changed gears, her elbow could easily bump into Robin's thigh. But they had to work on the friends part of their relationship first. And the word relationship wasn't even accurate, because Robin had clearly stated that she didn't do relationships.

While Micky drove, Robin told her about her impromptu trip to Seoul and how she'd had to deal with a bunch of bigoted men—once again.

"Sometimes I think my job could be done better by a man," Robin said. "Just to get past that initial barrier of contempt. Awful as that may sound."

But Micky had never been very concerned with things like feminism and equality in the workplace. She sure thought them important, but they didn't really apply to her life as, first, a stay-at-home mother and, now, a glorified waitress—she guessed she could get away with calling herself a barista, if pressed—at a very gay-friendly coffee shop.

"Are you out at work?" Micky asked when Robin had gone silent, probably contemplating a work issue she hadn't figured out yet. She recognized the look on her face from Darren. How on Friday night he was there in person but not yet in spirit. He always needed a few hours to shake the workweek off him.

"Of course I am." Robin looked at her. "I'm the Diversity Manager. What signal would it send to the people I'm trying to influence if I was in the closet?"

Wrong question. Though she enjoyed finding out about Robin's day-to-day life at Goodwin Stark, she was eager to change the topic of conversation to something lighter. Micky just nodded. At least she wasn't *only* thinking about ways to get Robin between the sheets as quickly as possible again.

"Funny thing," she said. "Darren, my ex-husband, told me yesterday that he's seeing someone who works for Goodwin Stark as well. Her name is Lisa. That's all I know."

To Micky's relief, Robin didn't instantly show signs of recognizing the name. "We have so many employees, and I tend to spend my time either with the top brass or people militant enough to join special task forces." Robin looked at Micky again. "Don't worry, your secret is safe with me." She put a hand on Micky's leg, causing Micky to almost lose control of the steering wheel for an instant.

✳ ✳ ✳

It was still early—Micky had insisted on picking up Robin before traffic to Bondi got too congested—and the beach wasn't busy yet. Micky had skipped breakfast, her stomach too up in arms about seeing Robin again, but was now experiencing insistent pangs of hunger.

"They have the best croissants over there." She pointed at a bakery she vaguely remembered going to years ago. Micky was not a Bondi beach kind of woman. Already, she saw two men who were so obviously—so ostentatiously—gay skipping along the boardwalk.

"Sure." Robin followed Micky to the small cluster of tables outside the bakery café.

After ordering and finding a spot overlooking the beach and ocean, Micky said, "God, I haven't been here in ages." She cast her glance over the vista in front of her and had to admit it was beautiful. "We lived close to the beach in Mosman. It was great for the kids," she mused, letting her guard down.

"I'm going to be honest with you." Robin painted a look on her face Micky couldn't quite figure out. "You're the first mother I've slept with. Not that I'm in any way discriminatory against mothers, but you know, they're just not a kind of lesbian I come across often."

Micky's brain was already going into overdrive. Robin had just called her a lesbian. How politically incorrect was that? Surely, after having told her about being married to Darren for eighteen years, someone like Robin, someone who had to deal with insensitivity and prejudice in her job all the time, would at least assume Micky was bisexual.

"I'm sorry. Did I say something wrong?" Robin asked.

Micky tried to rearrange her features and look less vexed, but she figured it wasn't really working. "That's the first time I've been referred to as a lesbian. A bit of a leap seeing as I've only slept with a woman once." Thankfully, Micky kept her voice from wavering.

"Oh, I didn't mean it like that. I was more speaking in general. I wouldn't want to presume anything about you. Though I am curious as to how you see yourself?"

The question was bound to come at Micky—hard and fast—at some point. If she'd allowed herself more time to think this through, instead of being carried away by images of Robin's hand on her breast and her face disappearing between her legs, perhaps Micky would have an answer. But who was she kidding? Micky had had an entire lifetime to think this through. More time was not what she needed. She just needed to stop being so afraid.

Micky shook her head. Amber had, in many different ways, tried to coax an answer to this question from her, but this was not Amber sitting across from her. This was Robin.

"I don't consider myself a lesbian." Micky remembered the word *latebian* she had picked up in that magazine. "I guess I'm… questioning."

Robin made a guttural sound in the back of her throat and just nodded. Perhaps she was expecting more of an actual answer. Micky felt compelled to fill the silence caused by Robin's lack of reply.

"Sleeping with a woman once at the age of forty-four hardly makes me a lesbian." There was the defensiveness again. Amber had called her out on it many a time. Micky didn't know why she just couldn't have a relaxed conversation about this. This was her life, after all. One of the most important aspects of it. It was, whether she openly admitted to it or not, one of the reasons she had left Darren.

"I'm not asking you to label yourself," Robin said. "I'm

just curious, just trying to find out what makes you tick."

You, Micky wanted to shout. *Your lips on mine, your hands on my skin.* How could she be overflowing with this kind of lust, yet, at the same time, unable to admit what was so obvious. Because it was complicated. That had always been Micky's go-to answer when questioned by Amber.

"I'm gay, Micky," Amber used to say. "Nothing you tell me will even remotely shock me."

It was the word *shock* that got to Micky the most. Because she had shocked herself. And if she did at some point come out, tell someone using actual words and her voice, say it out loud, what would that make her and the life she had lived so far? Micky remembered the spectrum Amber had talked about. How things can change over time. She might have been besotted with Darren when they married, but there was one thing she could state with clear certainty: not even at the height of their happiness, had sex with Darren come close to that one night with Robin.

Though, of course, Micky could come up with all sorts of logical explanations for that as well. When she and Darren first got together, she was in her early twenties and nowhere near the peak of her sexuality. Robin had just caught her at the right time: sex-deprived and at an age when, if women's magazines were to be believed, her sexuality was blossoming like never before.

"All I can tell you at this point is that I sure wouldn't mind repeating what happened last Tuesday." *Wow*. Had Micky actually just said that? She guessed it was a case of her lips overflowing with what her heart was full of—or at least a slew of other body parts.

"This is exactly what makes you so intriguing to me." Robin pinned her gaze on Micky, stared at her for a long while without so much as blinking. "To me, it's so clear that you do know what you want, but you have all this inner turmoil going on, which I understand." She leaned over the table. "I was in bed with you, Micky. I know. You didn't lie when we were between the sheets, when you were kissing me, when you slipped your hand… there."

Micky was terrified and aroused at the same time. But Robin wasn't finished analyzing Micky just yet.

"When I say I usually don't come across women like you, I mean in my personal life. Having worked in severely repressed regions in Asia, I have, of course, met many women and men so deep in the closet, just meeting me, an openly gay woman, made them break out into a cold sweat. It's confrontational. It made them face the one thing about themselves they couldn't come to grips with. I think I have the same effect on you. And of course there's the tiny matter of us sleeping together."

Micky sat up a bit straighter. She felt put on the spot but also, strangely, understood on a level Amber never did. "Why did you ask me out and sleep with me?"

"Because I was attracted to you and I'm used to following my instincts." Robin said it as though it were the most obvious statement ever made.

Micky wanted to ask, *Me? You were attracted to me?* Not that she considered herself unattractive in general, but compared to Robin and, she imagined, compared to the kind of women Robin usually slept with, she considered herself dowdier, more homely than attractive. Though, of course, Micky had no idea of the kind of woman Robin usually courted. She was getting curious about Michelle, Robin's Hong Kong non-girlfriend.

When Micky didn't say anything, Robin continued. "I don't have relationships out of necessity, or at least, that's how I've always seen it. It could of course also be because I never met *that* woman, but this arrangement I have with myself suits me just fine. Knowing that you're experimenting and trying to find yourself, so to speak, doesn't faze me for that very reason, Micky. I think we can have some good fun together."

"No strings attached." Micky repeated the phrase

Robin had used the previous week.

"And no rules." Robin stared straight ahead of her. "What do you say we go and have some fun on the beach?"

CHAPTER FOURTEEN

As far as beach days went, this one was a rather uncomfortable one for Micky. Not because of the growing crowds as time crept more toward midday or the sand that invariably got stuck in places she didn't want it to, but because every time she looked at Robin, in her glorious, flawless bikini body—outlined abs, muscled thighs, toned shoulder-line—she felt something twinge in the pit of her stomach. Something she didn't recognize because she really didn't want to. She didn't want to acknowledge that spending time with Robin made her feel more alive than she had in a decade. That lying next to her, uncomfortably, on a beach towel while staring into the surf, made her feel things she had never felt before. Things that were taking her whole being by storm.

Was she experimenting? She pondered that question in the moments when Robin had her eyes closed and their conversation stalled. Hell yeah, she was. But there was more to it than that. No strings attached and no rules was all well and good, but it also implied that no feelings other than being friends could blossom here, and how on earth was Micky supposed to stop that?

"Penny for your thoughts," Robin said, glancing at Micky with one eye open and the other squeezed shut.

By then, they'd gone into the water twice—its temperature a little too chilly for Micky's taste, though it didn't seem to bother Robin—and Robin had, with deft but oh, so sensuous strokes, smeared sunscreen on Micky's back.

"The crowd's getting a bit too thick for my taste."

Micky grabbed her chance. "How about we get out of here?"

Robin didn't say anything, not with words anyway, just plastered a big grin on her face and nodded. Instantly, deep inside of Micky, that fire started up again. The one that had been stoked the moment Robin had approached her at The Pink Bean and, so very unexpectedly, made a move on her.

In the car, Micky's entire body seemed to turn into one ultrasensitive synapse. It felt as though Robin was already stroking her—she could still feel the press of Robin's thumb under her shoulder blade where she'd applied sunscreen to her back earlier. Micky was getting ready for that big plunge into headiness and sexiness and that other world she'd discovered, that existed parallel to the one she'd been inhabiting for forty-four years but had been too afraid to visit—or even acknowledge its existence.

It was a long drive back to Darlinghurst, though most traffic was going in the opposite direction. They passed cars with surfboards strapped to the roof, with people chatting and laughing behind the wheel. When they crossed a car with a husband and wife in the front and two children in the back, and Micky glanced at it for a while longer in the rearview mirror, her foot firmly on the gas pedal, it felt as though she was, rapidly and unstoppably, driving away from her past.

Micky wanted so very much to listen attentively to what Robin was saying about the vast differences between Sydney and Hong Kong. She caught fragments of sentences like "less frenetic," "more humane," and "a million fucking times more friendly," but Micky couldn't possibly focus her attention on Robin's words. She was in a state of expectation, of wanting what was going to happen next so badly—of needing it as though her life depended on it—that she was afraid that if she let her eye off the ball, if she didn't keep driving the way she was, propelling them in the direction of her house, where she would finally be able to take off her clothes and meet Robin skin-to-skin and become that woman again that Robin had made her, that the moment would pass. That it wouldn't happen. That Robin, and all the things she stood for, would slip through her fingers.

"Your place or mine?" Micky asked when they reached the outskirts of Darlinghurst. She was so wrapped up in images of her and Robin, brimming with lust and unbridled desire—a state so intoxicating, she should decidedly not be driving—that the notion of them going their separate ways after this day at the beach didn't even exist in her mind.

"You haven't been listening to a word I've been saying, have you?" Robin placed her hand on Micky's knee.

"Fuck it, Robin. I want you so much. You have no idea." Micky was done with pretense, with keeping her desire locked away behind a veil of decency.

"Let's go to yours. I'd like to see it."

Micky stepped on the gas a little more.

★ ★ ★

"Nice place," Robin said, casting an appreciative glance around.

Micky had foreseen this particular scenario of bringing Robin home and had done a quick cleaning swoop of the living room that morning before leaving. Anyway, her small house was always much tidier when the kids weren't there.

It was unsettling to see Robin standing in her living room—another reason why she'd had to move. Micky could never have brought a woman into the living room of her old house, the house she'd lived in with Darren for so many years, and where her children had grown from babies to toddlers into teenagers. That was a different time, a different life, a different Michaela Ferro.

Because there she stood, heart thumping, with another woman in her house, ready to pounce on her. Last Tuesday, Micky had felt too overwhelmed to take the initiative, but today she was up for it, as though one night with Robin had been enough to give her a crash course in the secrets of lesbian—there was that word again—lovemaking.

Micky didn't thank Robin for the compliments on how she had decorated her house. Instead, she bridged the gap between them and threw her arms around Robin's neck, drawing her near. She hoped that the kiss she pressed on Robin's lips said it all: that she'd wanted to do that all day, all week—all her life.

"Do you want to take a shower?" Robin whispered in her ear when they broke from that first kiss that left Micky dizzy and wanting so much more.

Micky shook her head, took Robin by the hand, and dragged her up the stairs. She didn't have time for showers— though a possible scenario for extreme hotness did present itself there. But she wanted Robin spread wide for her as soon as possible, right that minute. She couldn't leap up the stairs fast enough.

As nerve-racking as that first date with Robin had been, it had served its purpose. Micky didn't have time for nerves anymore right then. The hours she'd already spent with Robin today, and how they had made her arousal grow out of proportion, had freed her of all inhibitions. Micky didn't worry about wanting to impress Robin anymore. She had so much zeal, desire, and pure lust on her side, it would be impossible not to please her. It was as much a given as how, at that very moment, just before Micky was about to tear her clothes off her, Micky realized that, yes, she was, indeed, very much a lesbian.

When the heart *and* the loins worked in tandem like this, there was no longer any use denying anything. Micky was overcome by not only lust but also by an emotion so pure and raw in its intention, she didn't want to lie to herself anymore. She didn't want to lie to anyone anymore—though that was a matter for later. The truth Micky was about to engage in now was much easier to express. It consumed her, made her fingertips tingle when they touched Robin's skin, made her heart leap when their lips met.

Micky didn't give Robin a chance to appraise her sparsely decorated bedroom—there was only space for a bed, a nightstand, and a small wardrobe. Micky had downsized in every aspect of her life after her divorce, except in the emotions department, as though she needed to cast off her former excess of belongings to become this person focused much more on her inner world. She kissed Robin fully on the lips again and, in the brief moments that they broke apart, tugged off her shorts and hoisted her top over her arms, flinging them both somewhere on the hardwood floor.

"Someone's eager," Robin said, and took a step back, regarding Micky while a small smile played on her lips.

Was she going too fast? Putting Robin off? Micky was already down to her swimwear, had already brought her hands behind her back to unclasp her bikini top. Her skin was on fire, mimicking every cell inside of her.

"Take a deep breath," Robin said, sounding very much like Amber, which gave Micky the breathing room she needed. "Relax. I'm not going anywhere. We have all night."

While Micky liked the sound of that—particularly the implied promise that Robin would be staying the night—she couldn't stop herself. Her rational mind, the only part of her that was even willing to consider slowing down, had to contend with that fire inside of her, and really, one was no match for the other.

"I want you," Micky said. She didn't care if she was endlessly repeating herself, reduced to a dumbed-down body with a one-track mind. She had a lifetime of desire to catch up on. She felt it throb violently between her legs, felt her bikini bottoms flood with it.

"I can see that." Robin's smile diminished, her features growing more serious.

If Micky *was* going to take a breath, she would use that moment to drink in Robin's glorious face. Her blue eyes, her long lips, her hair tied back in a ponytail, leaving her shoulders free to be ogled. Micky didn't know what she had done in a previous life to have landed in bed with someone like Robin in this one. She didn't care, didn't believe in any of that, though the thought had crossed her mind. All she cared about was feeling those toned muscles twitch underneath her, Robin's flesh yielding to her touch. Micky had dreamed of this moment for ten days. It had been ten days since she'd woken up next to Robin and had had to dash out of her apartment. Ten days of pent-up desire, followed by spending a few hours next to a bikini-clad Robin on the beach. What had Sheryl and Kristin called it? Lesbian puberty? Oh yes, Micky was certainly in the throes of that.

Then, at last, Robin tugged her tank top over her head, wiggled out of her shorts.

Micky took it as a sign that she could now unsnap her bikini top. She tossed it to the floor with reckless abandon, as though the bikini coming off was the sign for her desire to unleash completely. She stepped out of her bikini bottoms and approached Robin, giving her an eager hand until they were both completely undressed. Micky dragged her onto the bed, wanted to feel the weight of Robin's naked body on top of her, wanted to revel in it.

Micky threw her arms around Robin, drew her near, their lips and tongue meeting at an increasingly frantic pace. All the desire Micky had had to keep inside came rushing to the surface. Ten days of foreplay. Micky hadn't dared call it that in her head, but now she realized that's what it had been. Was it going to be like this every week? Oh, fuck it, she didn't have time to think of that. Robin was pressing a deliciously smooth knee between her legs, against her naked sex, and Micky responded by slanting her entire body in the direction of that knee.

Micky's hands groped hungrily and greedily. She brought one of them between their writhing bodies and grabbed for one of Robin's magnificent breasts. The other, more daring, scooted down in search of Robin's wetness.

Robin kissed her lips, neck, lips again, her mouth now drifting to Micky's ear, and gently planted her teeth into Micky's earlobe. Then she pushed herself away from Micky for an instant, allowing them both to catch a breath. A wicked grin crept along her face. Micky couldn't wait to find out what it meant. Robin pushed herself all the way up until she sat on her haunches and then, in one swift motion, turned herself around, straddling Micky and backing up to her, bum-first.

Oh Christ.

Robin's strong body moved swiftly and lightly along Micky's, until her pussy was—and there really was no other way to describe it—in Micky's face. Micky could only conclude that Robin had read her eagerness, because how could it not have come across loud and clear? Now there she lay, trapped underneath Robin, staring straight at her most intimate parts.

Unafraid, and overtaken by a new level of lust, Micky brought her hands to Robin's ass cheeks, let her nails dig into the soft flesh of them while, tentatively at first, her tongue darted out of her mouth and found Robin's pussy.

Just as her tongue made contact, she felt Robin's tongue between her own legs. Micky's legs stiffened for an instant, her body adjusting to the overload of sensuality being bestowed upon it. But this was exactly what she wanted. All of it. Her tongue on Robin while Robin's explored her. It made Micky bolder, made her insert her tongue deeper, with more strength and intention. She licked along Robin's wet, wet lips, sucked them into her mouth, lapped at her lover's pussy as if there was no tomorrow.

The double action of licking Robin and being licked by her at the same time made Micky ready to be tipped over the edge any second now. The smoldering sensation beneath her skin was quickly turning into full-blown fireworks, and she had more and more trouble focusing her tongue on the task at hand. Then, Robin brought a finger into the mix. She pushed into Micky slowly but steadily, and despite Micky's desire for Robin to feel the exact same thing as she was in that divine moment, she soon lost all her focus to the obliterating, inevitable orgasm coursing through her, claiming her. Her head fell back into the pillow, while Robin fucked and licked her, and everything went black in Micky's brain for an instant, followed by a bright explosion of pure whiteness.

When she came to, Robin's pussy was no longer offered to Micky the way it had been before. Instead, Robin had swiftly pirouetted back to face Micky and now sat straddling Micky's belly.

"What the hell are you doing to me?" Micky stammered, not even having the wherewithal to feel self-conscious about asking such a silly question. Because it was clear what Robin was doing to her. She was making great strides in the conquest of Micky's body—and heart.

Robin didn't reply. Just smiled down at Micky, scooted closer—Micky could feel the wetness of her pussy leaving a trail on her belly, then her breasts—until her pussy was wholly on offer once again.

I'm covered in woman. She dug her nails into Robin's backside and pulled her as close as she possibly could without losing the ability to breathe. She delved her tongue into Robin's pussy and continued where she'd left off before the orgasm had swept through her. When she opened her eyes for an instant, she had a clear view of Robin's perky breasts and, beyond them, of her exposed neck while she threw her head back in, what Micky hoped, was burgeoning ecstasy.

Micky gave it all she had. She alternated applying pressure with her tongue and bestowing the lightest of flicks on Robin's clit and, meanwhile, relished how Robin's body squirmed on top of hers. Micky was basically trapped between Robin's thighs and, though she'd never envisioned an exact scenario like this one, took great delight in it. Then she remembered the effect the addition of a finger to the action had had on her earlier. She wiggled an arm underneath Robin's thigh, pulled her mouth back from that intoxicating pussy for an instant, and plunged a finger inside Robin's hot, moist depths.

"Oh God," Robin exclaimed. "Oh yes."

A brand new source of fire ignited under Micky's skin. The receiving and the giving, the endless cycle of it made her curl her toes in anticipation as well. They had all night to repeat this, over and over again. And tomorrow was Sunday.

As Robin's thighs clamped themselves around Micky's head almost savagely, a rush of happiness burrowed itself through her flesh. All it took was for Micky to be wholly covered in woman to experience this kind of freeing satisfaction.

CHAPTER FIFTEEN

After Robin had so brazenly come to sit on Micky's face, changing Micky's perception of herself a little more once again, they took a shower and went out to dinner. Micky didn't remember much of dinner because her brain was so filled to the brim with all things Robin—her fingers, her wet sex, her wicked grin—that it seemed as though there was no room left in her short-term memory to store new impressions.

After dinner, there was a moment where, in hindsight, the perfect day they had spent together could have gone awry, when Micky saw a flicker of hesitation creep along Robin's features when she asked if she was coming back home with her to spend the night.

In the end, after a brief moment of having to think about it, Robin said, "Why the hell not?" and they walked to Micky's house together. The only reason Micky didn't grab Robin's hand on the short walk was not because she didn't want to be seen holding another woman's hand in her new neighborhood, but because she didn't know if holding hands in public was within the boundaries of their friends-with-benefits arrangement.

They had tried to watch the news on TV, but Robin's proximity, and the fact that they had the house all to themselves, made Micky unable to focus. She couldn't keep her hands off Robin, was always touching at least one fingertip to her skin.

"Do you want to talk?" Robin asked at one point, but Micky just shook her head.

She'd never been the kind of girl to indulge in drugs, even a joint had always been too much for her non-smoker lungs, but she imagined this was what it felt like to lose control of her faculties. To have dopamine rush after dopamine rush cloud the working of the brain and reduce a person to a recurrent pleasure-seeker. But just for tonight, Micky didn't care. Her brain might be fogged over with lust and dreaminess and foreign-to-her chemical processes, somewhere in the back of it, the realization did sit that she would be worrying about all of this later. About the consequences of this day on her life. That's why, on this Saturday evening, and well into the night, until the moment Robin would kiss her good-bye, Micky would allow herself all the indulgence she had denied herself for years.

Micky kneeled between Robin's legs downstairs in the living room sofa. Afterward, Robin pushed her against her bedroom door when they went up to sleep. Micky was so exhausted, her body too drained to leave any energy for her mind to worry, that she slept so deeply and late that the sun was already streaming through the windows when she woke up.

To her instant relief, because in the brief instant between opening her eyes and turning her body to look she'd feared the worst, Robin was still there. She lay curled into a ball with her back to Micky, hogging most of the sheet.

Micky fell back onto the mattress, letting all the memories of the day before flood her brain. How could she possibly resume her life after a day like that? How could she face her children? She was lucky they were both in a phase of their teenage years that had them mainly focused on themselves. Perhaps they wouldn't notice how, overnight, Micky had changed.

And there was that word again: lesbian. Micky figured she had moved quite a bit on the spectrum in the space of one day. Even if she hadn't reached full-blown lesbianism on the scale just yet, she'd at least engaged in some very lesbian activity. And she had enjoyed every single second of it. But this morning, in the clear light of day, she would have to face the consequences. She would need Amber. But, perhaps, before all of that… She turned on her side and ran a finger over Robin's magnificent back. Even from this point of view, she was beautiful. Irresistible.

Micky remembered those nights in college when she would drink so much that, the next day when she woke up after a few hours of sleep, she'd still feel intoxicated. That was how she felt now. She wasn't silly enough to think that this was love, but Micky was surely—unequivocally—in lust.

Robin stirred and rolled onto her back, displaying her ample chest to Micky's gaze. There was no more doubt in Micky's mind that they were real. After two pregnancies, Micky's own breasts, compared to Robin's, looked a little sad, but instead of comparing herself to Robin's younger, worked-out body, Micky had told herself to enjoy it. After all, Robin had repeatedly said that she would be leaving Sydney at the end of the year. Micky had to take full advantage of the time she was there, and she would worry about the shape of her own body later, once Robin had left.

What an excruciating thought. Robin leaving.

"Morning." Robin opened her eyes and stretched her arms over her head.

"Hey." When she looked into Robin's sleep-crusted eyes like that, Micky did, for a split second, wonder if she'd only fallen in lust. If this wasn't more already. But how could it be? If it was, then she was just projecting or it was some other psychological trick her brain was playing on her. People in puberty fell in love in a flash. That was what was happening to her. Lesbian puberty.

"What time is it?" Robin grabbed Micky's hand.

"A bit after ten."

"No CrossFit again for me today. You're ruining my fitness." Robin smiled while lifting both their hands in the space between them.

"You're improving mine." Micky's heart flooded with a strange sensation. What could possibly be more heavenly than to wake up next to another woman on a Sunday morning?

"What are you doing today?" Robin kept playing with Micky's hand.

"Not much. Possibly meet up with Amber."

"What would you do if I weren't here?"

"Exactly the same, plus feel sorry for myself because you weren't here." Micky didn't stop the impulse to press a kiss to Robin's cheek. Granted, she didn't know much about the whole friends-with-benefits thing, but she knew this was not it. This scene, in her bedroom on a glorious Sunday morning, was not one of a couple of friends having just spent the night together and happily, freely, and with a few friendly orgasms in their pockets, going on their way, continuing their lives as though this had no impact on their souls.

"Well, I'm here so no need to feel sorry for yourself." When Robin smiled, the first pinch of dread settled in Micky's stomach. Already, she was feeling anxious about the moment Robin would leave, when they would say good-bye —awkwardly, most likely, because Micky wouldn't know what to say.

"Do you want to make another friend?" she asked. "You met Amber briefly at The Pink Bean last week. I'm pretty sure she would love to get to know you better."

"Because I'm fucking her best friend?" Robin trapped Micky's hand between hers and the spot just below her naked breast.

"Well, yes, if you put it like that." *Speaking of fucking.*

"I don't know if it's a good idea. Yesterday and last night were great fun." Robin gave Micky's hand a little squeeze. "But maybe we should talk instead of being formally introduced to friends."

Micky remembered Robin asking her if she wanted to

talk last night, but talk had been the very last thing on her mind. It still was now, but for a different reason. Any conversation they would have now would ruin the spell she was under, these blissful moments of complete ignorance, of being another, brand new version of Michaela Ferro. Moreover, Micky knew she *needed* to have the conversation, lest she lose control over her feelings even more. Her lusty brain had to be put in its place—but the renewed throbbing between her legs wasn't helping.

"What do you want to talk about?" Micky's voice sounded too petulant to her liking, but she couldn't take back the tone she'd said the words in.

"I know that yesterday I said there were no rules, but for this to work, I think we will need some, anyway."

"Why can't it just be what it is, without having to say it's this or that? Why can't we just enjoy each other's company?" Micky withdrew her hand from Robin's grasp and let herself fall onto her back.

"To avoid exactly what is happening now." Robin pushed herself up on an elbow. "I've told you…"

"Yes, yes, I know. You don't do relationships, and you're leaving at the end of the year." It's only March, Micky wanted to add, with great emphasis.

"I just don't want there to be any misunderstandings between us." Robin's voice was kind, as were her eyes on Micky.

"What rules would you even have?" Micky was the one who grabbed for Robin's hand now. She needed to feel her touch, feel connected to her. "In all these years you've lived abroad, have you never… fallen in love?"

"I have, Micky, and then I had to leave. That's why I can't let it happen again."

"How do you even do that? It's not as if it's an emotion you can just turn off."

"By having rules and being vigilant."

Micky shook her head. "But I want to fall in love. By

God, I want it so much. I want to feel what I felt with you last night again and again. I don't want to be vigilant and have rules about how I'm allowed to feel. I'm too old for that. I've wasted too much time. I just want to live and try to be happy. Now that we're having this talk, I'm not interested in being friends with benefits either. I think it's a ridiculous concept." Micky looked away from Robin. She could feel her pulse in her throat, throbbing like crazy, as though rooting for her after what she'd just said.

Next to her, Robin sighed. "Then I only have one choice," she said. "I need to take a step back."

Micky wasn't done. She imagined all the words that were spilling out of her right now having piled up in her brain over the past twenty-four hours. Shoved to the side, deemed inappropriate for the moment, until they were too many and came bursting out.

"Why? Why are you like this, Robin? You claim you just want to have fun, yet you suck the fun right out of it with your talk of rules and vigilance. How can you live like that?"

"Because…" Robin pursed her lips together. "I don't want there to be an imbalance between us. I don't want you to feel more for me than I can give back and vice versa."

"What does that even mean?" Micky sat up straighter.

"I'll tell you what it means. And I know you'll know what I'm talking about." Robin fixed her gaze on Micky. "I know because there's something between us. Something different. Something that, if we don't pay attention, will turn into much more than the spark it is now."

"But isn't that just the most wonderful thing about it?" Micky threw her hands up in exasperation. Of course, she knew what Robin was trying to say, but she did not want to hear those words. "Look." She placed a hand on Robin's thigh. "I just celebrated the one-year anniversary of my divorce. I loved my husband, but I would be lying if I said we had a speck of passion left for the past… ten years. There was nothing. Nada. Zilch. Then I met you, and you

114

reintroduced me to what passion really feels like. As though all the passion I had missed out on during the last decade of my life had been compressed in the little time I've spent with you. And yes, that's going to have an impact on me, is going to leave me feeling like a hormonal lesbian-in-puberty, but fuck it, Robin, this"—she pointed at the two of them with widespread fingers—"is exactly what I want. I couldn't have dreamed of it, but now that I've experienced it, I know it's what I want."

"I can't give you what you want." Robin's voice didn't have a lot of smile left in it.

"But you've already given it to me." That pinch of dread in Micky's stomach was quickly turning into a vise grip of despair around her heart.

"Then it looks like I will have to take it back." Robin just sat there motionless, making Micky believe she still had a chance to convince her otherwise.

"What are you so afraid of? I don't understand. What could be more glorious than this?" Of course, Micky could refer to how she felt all she wanted, that didn't mean Robin felt the same.

"I'm not afraid." More steel in Robin's voice. "I had wrongly assumed we were on the same page, what with you barely being out, but I see now that I made an error of judgment."

"An error of judgment? That's what you're calling me?"

Robin shook her head. "Can't you see? What is happening now is exactly the sort of thing I try to avoid. I don't need this sort of drama."

"Oh, sure, next thing you'll tell me you don't need love in your life either." Oh shit. Micky hadn't meant to say the l-word. That was a grave mistake. She blamed the pile of words rapidly rushing from the back to the front of her brain.

"Micky, Micky, Micky." Robin started shifting under the sheets. "I think I'd better go."

"Fine." Micky could kick herself for saying what she had about love. It wasn't even relevant. Though she stood by all the other things she'd said. "Go."

"I'm sorry this is not working out the way you had hoped. I really thought I had been clear from the very beginning." Obviously, Robin was not the storming-out-in-a-huff kind and liked to have the last word. "I truly am sorry."

"I don't even know what we're fighting about." Micky tried to sound as aloof as possible. "We've only just met. I'm just a lonely divorcée discovering her true feelings for women for the very first time. Don't mind little old me." That sounded much more like self-pity than aloofness. Robin made Micky pick all the wrong words from the jumble in her mind.

"I like you, Micky. Otherwise, I wouldn't still be here. I would have gone home last night. Come to think of it, that's what I should have done. That was my bad. But this… useless arguing over feelings, that's something I don't do. And yes, you absolutely deserve someone who will fall madly in love with you. And you will find that woman soon enough, I promise you. You have a knack for attracting them, take it from me."

What did that even mean? Why didn't Robin just go home already instead of messing with Micky's head more.

"But I can tell you one thing with absolute certainty: I am not the woman you're looking for." With that, Robin did get up and start searching for the clothes she had so easily, so willingly and eagerly, discarded the previous night, before hopping into bed with Micky for the second time in one day.

Now Micky's brand new bed was tainted with the memory of all that they had done in it; and the different person Micky had become in the process: free, curious, exhilarated.

She watched as Robin amassed her clothes and hurried into the bathroom. I guess that shower Micky had dreamed of the two of them taking together was now out of the question.

She could get up, fight some more, try to articulate her thoughts better, but she knew there was no use. Additionally, what right did she have to put any claims on Robin? She was just in lust, any logical thoughts clouded by the new memories she had made and the acute desire to be covered in woman all over again as soon as possible.

The problem, at this very moment, was that Micky couldn't possibly imagine that woman being anyone but Robin.

CHAPTER SIXTEEN

"Jesus, Amber, I'm so stupid." Amber was the only person in the world Micky would admit something like that to. But it was exactly how she felt. Utterly stupid. "I should have just kept my mouth shut."

"I disagree. You should say what you feel. What was the alternative?"

"Er, amazingly hot sex." Micky could barely look her friend in the eye.

"But at what cost?"

"Cost? I have no price to pay here. I have so many years to catch up on, and I had the most exquisite, experienced, enthralling woman in bed, just mere hours ago, and I let her go because of my feelings."

"Come on, Micky. We are not animals. We can't just make love and move on."

Having Amber as a best friend was a blessing and a curse. Amber never—ever—slept with anyone until their chakras were aligned. "You were the one who told me to do this, if I may be so frank as to remind you." Micky opened an expensive bottle of wine, which she'd snatched from Darren's collection after he'd moved out, and drank greedily. "You encouraged some mindless fucking." Micky also hadn't had breakfast or lunch. She knew as soon as she said the word Amber wouldn't react well to the f-word.

"I did no such thing. All I advised you to do was to be open to possibilities, which you were. And I applaud you for that. I also think you did the right thing. So did Robin. These things happen, Micky. People have different expectations of one situation most of the time. But this was your first. It would have been pretty naive to believe you were going to fall in love with the first woman you met who tickled your fancy, and end up happily ever after. This is life, not a fairy tale."

"I know." This was the blessed part of her friendship with Amber. "I just really, really like her."

"Which is the problem," Amber stated matter-of-factly.

"I think she likes me too. I think *that*'s the problem."

"I know this is not what you want to hear right now, but you're going to have to move on."

"I know." If only Micky knew how. Then she imagined Robin moving on. The thought of running into her with another woman by her side made her stomach roil.

"Either way, I would advise you to play the field, Micky. Your first steps into this brave new world"—only Amber would ever call what Micky had done by that dramatic name —"were glorious. It would be so easy to put a positive spin on it. Remember my first time with Annette Fielding?" Amber fixed her green gaze on Micky. "You're lucky."

"Wasn't your first time with Steven What's-His-Name?" Micky said, knowing full well she would rile Amber greatly with that comment.

"My real first time." Amber didn't even raise her voice. Maybe she'd been doing yoga all weekend and she was so Zen nothing Micky said could rattle her.

"I just feel…" Micky was starting to get sick of feeling sorry for herself. What was it that Amber always said? *Introspection is fine. Wallowing is not.* "Like I've wasted so much time."

"Though I understand that sentiment, you could also choose to look at things differently. You used your time to build a family, and it gave you two beautiful children—and your best friend two beautiful godchildren. And you do have time, Micky. Time to discover yourself, to find out what you want. There's no ticking clock here."

"I've been thinking about the spectrum a lot," Micky said. "Honestly, after the time I spent with Robin, I can't possibly imagine ever falling for a man again."

"There's absolutely nothing wrong with that." Amber put a hand on Micky's arm, after which Micky proceeded to tell her about Darren's new girlfriend Lisa.

"Now you can stop feeling guilty about that as well. Darren has someone new in his life. He's moving on."

"It's just that when he told me about her and I imagined having to tell him and the kids about the new person in my life, it seemed very unfathomable. Like he would never be able to believe it."

Amber looked at her and didn't say anything for a few long seconds, then cleared her throat. "I never told you this because I promised I wouldn't, and I shouldn't even tell you now, although I think the term for keeping it a secret has passed, and I also think you need to know."

Micky's pulse picked up.

"After you first told him you wanted a divorce, Darren came to me. He was actually waiting for me outside the yoga studio, insisting on a chat. We went for a drink, and he asked me flat-out if, firstly, I knew what was going on and, secondly, if you'd ever shown signs of being attracted to women."

Micky's jaw slacked; her eyes widened. "He—he did?"

She couldn't believe Amber had never told her. Then again, anyone, even someone she'd never met before, who swore Amber to secrecy would get it, no questions asked. But this was Darren. And Amber was her best friend.

"The number of times I've wanted to tell you, but I couldn't. I hope you understand that." Amber patted Micky's arm.

"What did you reply?" Micky was trying to process this new piece of information. Had Darren known before she did?

"I told him the truth. I told him that I didn't know."

"Even though you did…"

Amber shook her head. "No, I didn't. You never really told me. Not that you had to, but you never said the words."

"Why do you think he asked you that question? Did you quiz him about that?" The fact that Darren might have suspected did not sit right with Micky, though, of course, for so many years, he had been the person she was closest to in her life. He was her husband. If it had been the other way around, surely she would have suspected something as well. Yet, he never expressed his suspicions to her.

Amber pondered this question for an instant. "He said it was just a feeling he got sometimes. I think he was just feverishly looking for answers at the time. Leaving no stone unturned."

"He was a good man, and I hurt him." No matter how happy Lisa made Darren, and it was absolutely not a given that she would, Micky would always feel guilty about that.

"You had no choice. That's just how it is sometimes."

"I should have told him. I should have been brave enough to address the real reason why I was tearing our family apart."

"How could you when you couldn't even admit it to yourself? At the very least you can thank Robin for that. But it took you a year after your divorce was actually finalized to take a step in the right direction. No one can ever blame you for jumping headlong into something you didn't think through for a very long time beforehand."

"Which is exactly why I feel like such a royal screw-up sometimes. How could I not have known? My best friend since childhood is a lesbian, for Pete's sake."

"Because it's different for all of us. There is no one prescribed path. It's a really hard thing to come to terms with for someone in your position. You should never, ever feel bad about walking your own path, Micky. Besides, look at you now. You know now."

"Do you think I should tell Darren?"

"In time, but first, you need to take the time it takes to accept it fully yourself."

"You mean sleep with some more women?" Micky could do with a chuckle right about now.

"If that's what it takes." Of course, Amber didn't take it as a joke.

Suddenly, another question reared its head. "Do you think Mom suspects?"

Amber scrunched her lips together. "That I truly can't answer. She's your mother and you're close, so she might, but she's never asked me about it."

"What are my children going to say when I tell them?" This was why coming to the realization that most of her life had been based on a desire she'd always carefully stowed away was so hard for Micky. All this informing of people she loved she would have to go through.

"Olivia and Christopher have the coolest lesbian aunt. And they're children of their time. They'll get used to it." Amber shot her an encouraging smile. "You're not required to tell anyone unless you feel 100 percent ready. Coming out, though an outward action, is deeply personal and should never be forced upon anyone."

"What would I do without you?" Micky looked her friend in the eye.

"My guess is you'd be going out for a good amount of beer and fish and chips tonight, which are, decidedly, not the answer to any of life's problems. I'm taking you out to dinner. You need some good food in you. I'll even meditate with you, if you were to feel so inclined."

"Don't push it," Micky said, looking at Amber. Despite missing Robin's presence enormously, she felt loved nonetheless.

CHAPTER SEVENTEEN

Micky was sitting with Kristin in The Pink Bean after her shift, waiting for Sheryl, who had the afternoon off, to join them for lunch. It was Tuesday, and Robin hadn't come in yet this week to order a wet capp. She'd probably found another coffee shop; the neighborhood was full of excellent ones. When Kristin had asked Micky if she wanted to join her and Sheryl for lunch, Micky had jumped at the opportunity—especially when she'd heard Kristin's erudite wife would be there.

Though she'd been quite liquored-up at the dinner party two weeks prior, Micky had taken an instant liking to well-spoken and straight-forward Sheryl. She looked forward to spending time with her while neither one of them were under the influence. Moreover, Olivia and Christopher, whom she had missed disproportionally since her last conversation with Robin, were only due back tomorrow. The last thing Micky needed was more time alone with her thoughts.

"Give it to me, boss," she joked, while sitting across from Kristin. "What's my performance report after three weeks? I know I lost you a loyal customer, but I'm glad we've discussed that already." Micky wasn't certain about Kristin's sense of humor. She was definitely the more serious one of the couple.

"You're doing fine." She fixed her dark eyes on Micky. "We both know I didn't give you the job because you graduated with honors from Barista School." She painted a wide smile on her face. "I recognize a woman in distress when I see one."

"That's very... altruistic of you. To put me before your business."

Kristin held up her hands. "I did no such thing. Customers will always come first, and I watched you like a hawk the first few days. You have a certain way with customers that not a lot of people have. That's much more important to me than knowing how to artfully pour a wet cappuccino." Kristin did have a sense of humor then.

"I really appreciate you taking me on. It was a steep learning curve, but I actually enjoy being here every morning."

"I can tell, which is why you get to stay."

"I'd like to have you and Sheryl over for dinner at my house some time soon. I can't promise the same culinary excellence you delivered, but I really enjoyed that dinner party you threw."

"About that..." Kristin got a wicked twinkle in her eye. "Do tell if it's too soon, but we have a friend we would like to introduce you to. She's a colleague of Sheryl's. Very smart, very accomplished and... kind of in a similar boat as you."

Micky's heart started hammering in her chest. Did they want to set her up? "I would surely not call myself accomplished," Micky joked, deflecting.

"No need to give me an answer now. Think about it. Let me know if and when you're ready. Meanwhile, we'd love to sample your cooking. Oh." Kristin sat up straighter. Micky had her back to the door. The first thought that flashed through her mind at Kristin's reaction was that Robin had walked in—that she'd waited until after Micky's shift to get her daily caffeine fix.

"There's Sheryl, and she's not alone." She bent over the table and found Micky's ear. "Trust me, this is not what we had agreed upon."

Confused, Micky rose and turned around. Sheryl smiled broadly at her. Next to her stood a woman with an equally winning smile. Then it dawned on Micky. It was the woman Kristin had just mentioned, and Sheryl had jumped the gun. Not a bad decision, Micky thought, because giving her the chance to ponder the possibility for too long would surely have resulted in a no.

"This is my colleague Martha," Sheryl said, "I've invited her to lunch. I hope you don't mind."

Martha was blonde like Robin, but in a very different way. Her hair color was eerily light, and surely real. She looked like she was from Eastern European descent with her high cheekbones and strong jaw. She was also at least ten years older than Robin.

Robin. Robin. Robin. Argh.

As Micky stretched out her hand, she vowed to stop comparing, push the memory of Robin to the back of her brain, and focus on getting to know Martha. After all, it wasn't every day that your boss's wife introduced you to *a woman in the same boat.*

Martha's grip was firm and cool, and she wasn't afraid to look Micky straight in the eye as they shook hands.

★ ★ ★

Micky couldn't believe she'd had such a hard time getting out of bed that morning. Look at her now. Her brand new friends had just set her up with a woman *and* she wasn't even freaking out about it. In fact, she welcomed the distraction Martha's inquisitive gaze brought.

On the way to the restaurant, Kristin and Sheryl walking ahead of her and Martha, Micky witnessed how they exchanged a few looks. Kristin was surely not the kind of person to scold her wife in public for introducing Micky to a potential love interest out of the blue like that, but Micky imagined she'd have a few things to say about it behind closed doors later.

Sitting down, Sheryl on one side of her, Martha on the other, Micky did feel a sort of accomplishment. A sentiment she could easily attribute to Amber again, for pushing her to work at The Pink Bean, and for recognizing that need for something more inside of her at the right time. But Micky was done selling herself short. She was the one who had had the courage to start working the morning shift at a coffee shop at the age of forty-four. An activity that, no matter the not-ideal outcome with Robin, had changed her life for the better.

"Just to get any misconceptions out of the way," Martha said solemnly after they'd ordered wine and water, "I was the one who asked Sheryl if I could join you for lunch."

An expert at disarming people. Then Micky was gripped by a bout of nerves. Why had Martha insisted?

"And here I was trying to set it all up subtly and slowly," Kristin replied. Underneath her stern Asian exterior, she was quite easygoing.

"It's fine," Micky said. "I feel flattered." Though, of course, aside from flattered, Micky also felt rather put on the spot. Was she supposed to start flirting with Martha in front of Sheryl and Kristin? Was it even okay to mention Robin now that they had introduced her to Martha? Micky would have liked to find out what Sheryl had to say about the whole Robin thing, but she could hardly ask her now.

"So do I." Martha fastened her gaze on Micky.

If this woman was, in fact, in the same boat as Micky, where did she get this amount of confidence?

Kristin and Sheryl were skilled at keeping the conversation going and asking the right kind of questions at the right time so Micky could give the gist of her story while she learned about Martha. After lunch, which had been civilized and pleasant, Micky knew that Martha fell into the same latebian category as she did, though her husband of twenty years had left her for "a younger model" first, before Martha'd had the chance to "realize her true potential." This information made Martha especially interesting to Micky, who left the restaurant with a million questions on her mind. To meet someone who was going through the same monumental changes was a relief.

Kristin and Sheryl discreetly disappeared after lunch, leaving Micky purposelessly lingering on the sidewalk with Martha.

"Dessert?" Martha asked.

Micky checked her watch. "I have yoga at four." Micky could not afford to miss today's class. She had too much inner turmoil to deal with—and renewed sexual energy to release—and she didn't want to disappoint Amber by not turning up again. "Which gives me forty-five minutes."

"I'll take them," Martha said.

★ ★ ★

"I have known for years," Martha said. "But when you're married to the Vice Chancellor at the University of Sydney, it's quite hard to just tell your husband and find yourself a lady."

"Until he left you." Micky was doing her best to remember Amber's words about every single person walking their very own particular path.

"I know it makes me sound like a coward, but it's not that simple. I have three children and two grandchildren."

"Hey, I hear you. I have two teenagers, and I know how complicated it all is." Micky sipped from her cappuccino, which still, invariably, made her think of Robin.

"Until we decide to un-complicate it."

"Do your children know?"

Martha nodded, then stared into her tea for a few moments. "My two sons barely batted an eyelid, but my daughter, the youngest, has taken it quite hard. We were always so close, and I think she feels betrayed more than anything. Because I wasn't honest with her."

"If you could turn back time, would you do things differently?" Micky was seriously considering skipping yoga. Having someone like Martha to talk to, someone who had already made her way out of the boat Micky was still stuck in, was invaluable.

Martha scoffed. "I wish I could give a resounding yes to that question, but I probably wouldn't have. Things were different thirty years ago. I married at the tender age of twenty. What did I know? If I compare that to all the things Stella, my daughter, has been subjected to in the first twenty years of her life already. There's a world of difference." She stared gloomily into her tea again.

"I don't mean to bombard you with questions." Micky suddenly became very aware of what she'd been doing, subjecting Martha to a questionnaire like that.

Martha waved her off. "It's okay, really. If I were you, I'd do the same. Having someone to talk to about these things plays such a crucial part. I have no idea where I would be right now if it weren't for Sheryl. Plus, I'm very interested in the details of your story." She gazed at Micky with that light stare again. "I know you have to run, but would you like to continue this conversation over a nice, long meal this weekend?"

"I would love that, but I have the kids this weekend."

"And you don't leave the house when they're home?" Martha's smile was crooked and inviting.

"I do, of course I do, but, er, well, you know…"

"I'm just teasing you, Micky. If anyone understands the predicament you're in, it's me. You don't want them to ask you annoying questions, and you don't want to lie to them. I get it."

"Can I think about it?" Micky wouldn't be lying if she told Olivia and Christopher she'd be having dinner with someone she met at the coffee shop. She also wanted to know their plans for the weekend first, before making plans of her own. "I'll let you know." It wouldn't even be a date. Martha didn't strike her as the kind of woman who thought in terms of going on a date. Micky just really wanted to pick her brain.

They exchanged numbers, pecked each other on the cheek lightly when they said goodbye, and on her way to yoga, Micky came to the conclusion that she hadn't thought about Robin all that much for the past forty-five minutes.

Just as Micky entered the changing room, her phone beeped. It was a message from Robin:

How about being just friends, no benefits?

CHAPTER EIGHTEEN

Micky still hadn't replied to Robin's message by the time she got to work the next morning. She hadn't been able to discuss it with Amber, who was teaching back-to-back classes and was attending a seminar on something Micky didn't really understand in the evening.

The reason Micky hadn't been able to bring herself to accept Robin's offer was because she simply couldn't imagine being just friends with her. The notion seemed so entirely out of the question that it seemed better to just avoid Robin altogether.

Until Robin stood right in front of her at The Pink Bean.

Josephine winked at Micky. Micky didn't keep her younger colleague up to speed on her private life, but the girl was no fool. "Feel free to take your break, Micky," she said. "I'll bring Robin's coffee over in a minute."

Faced with Robin like that, Micky knew exactly why she was to be avoided. All the images she'd been trying not to succumb to came rushing back. This, however, didn't mean that Micky wasn't happy to see Robin. Her heart was already doing that crazy pitter-patter thing again, and even her skin seemed to be reacting to Robin's sudden presence, the way it seemed to light on fire under Robin's blue gaze.

"I might have been a bit too harsh and principled," Robin said as soon as they'd sat down in the farthest corner of The Pink Bean. "I didn't mean to push you away like that."

Robin was dressed in work attire, her fitted blouse

clinging to her tight abdomen. Glancing at it, Micky realized that, if presented with the choice, she wanted the exact opposite of what Robin had proposed. One thing was for sure, however: she could not just be friends with Robin. It was out of the question.

"I've met someone," she blurted out. "Another woman." *Oh Christ.* Her brain was really not operating at its best. Micky blamed this entirely on Robin's scrumptious presence.

Robin cocked her head and looked at Micky intently. "You have? That's great."

Why had she even said that? To make Robin jealous? It wasn't a lie. Micky *had* met Martha—could even go on a date with her this weekend if she felt so inclined—but what she was conveying to Robin in no way matched how she felt about any of it. Because, come to think of it, and however much she wanted to pick Martha's brain for coming-out-later-in-life information, Micky would much rather spend any given evening with Robin than with Martha.

"Well, I mean, it's early days…" she stammered.

"I mean it, Micky. That's great. This will make it so much easier for us to be just friends." Robin made it sound as though all her dreams of friendship had just come true. Why was she so hell-bent on cultivating this friendship with Micky, anyway? Robin was the kind of person who could go to any bar on her own, sit there nursing a drink—even a ridiculous wet cappuccino—for ten minutes, and attract a crowd of strangers around her who would leave the venue eager to become her friend.

When Micky didn't say anything, Robin inquired further. "Tell me about this mystery woman." She quirked up her eyebrows and painted a hopeful smile on her face. "I have a few minutes before I have to leave for work."

In times of acute stress like this, Micky's go-to question had, over the years, become: what would Amber do? Of course, someone like Amber would never find herself in a situation like this, concocted of half-truths and un-communicated desires, but… what if she did? The reason Micky used Amber as a moral compass was because Amber made a point of always telling the absolute truth—except for that one time she didn't tell Micky about Darren questioning her sexuality.

"You're awfully quiet for someone who was so eager to tell me about the woman she just met," Robin said. "What's wrong?"

Micky sighed. The adrenalin rush of being faced with Robin was wearing off, making way for deflation. "I only just met her yesterday. I shouldn't have said that. I don't even know why I did."

"Why?" Robin looked at her the way, Micky guessed, she would at a life-long friend who was talking about her love life.

"*Why?*" Micky shuffled in her seat. "You can't come in here and pretend we're friends like that. It doesn't work that way."

"You're the one who told me about the other woman. I just presumed you wanted to talk about her."

Micky should just say the words that would make all of this much easier, but she couldn't bear to let them roll off her tongue. *You and I can't be friends.* "Look, I'm sorry, it's all been a bit much," she said instead—which was nothing but the truth.

"But you did meet someone?" Robin's tone was gentle. Maybe she was just curious—maybe she was even curious for the reason Micky wanted her to be.

"I did. Her name is Martha. She's a colleague of Sheryl's, Kristin's wife."

"And you want to see her again?" No matter how gentle her tone, Robin really wasn't letting it go.

"We'll see. Either way, I have the kids this weekend."

"So no chance of us doing anything together over the weekend?"

Micky knitted her brows together. "I really don't think that would be a good idea."

"We're just friends, remember?" Robin drank from her coffee but kept her eyes glued to Micky's. Did she even know she was giving a whole host of mixed signals?

The way things were going, Micky just wanted a quiet weekend at home. She had a job during the week now. She had to rest on Saturdays and Sundays. She didn't need all this innuendo and these *friendly* expectations. She would focus on the two most important people in her life: Olivia and Christopher.

"Yes, well, we'll work on our friendship the weekend after," she said firmly, then made to get up.

Robin grabbed her by the wrist and looked up at her. "Hey, have I done anything to upset you?"

Yes, Micky wanted to scream. *You rocked my world and then...* And then what? She couldn't fault Robin for a lack of honesty and transparency. It was her own feelings Micky had to deal with. Right now, faced with what felt like another rejection, Micky felt a ridiculous kind of anger stir in the pit of her stomach. Who did Robin think she was? Turning her on like that—basically changing her life—and then waltzing in here with a friendly smile on her face, casually asking about Martha as though what happened between them had no consequences for her whatsoever?

"No. I'll text you," Micky said. "I need to get back to work. Josephine's being swamped." They both looked at the counter where Josephine was cheerily chatting with Mark, one of the regulars. There was no queue.

"Okay." Robin let go of Micky's wrist and rose. "I'll see you tomorrow."

★ ★ ★

"So you want to be friends with Martha and more than friends with Robin, but the way things are presenting themselves, they both want the opposite," Amber said.

Micky hadn't contacted Martha or Robin. Instead, while

Christopher had decided to go to the beach to teach his new friend Liam how to surf and Olivia was *hanging out* with April, Micky sat on her tiny front porch with Amber, drinking a green juice.

"I don't know exactly what they want. I can only be sure of what I want." After seeing Robin at The Pink Bean for two subsequent days since their conversation on Wednesday, Micky had no doubts about what she wanted. She'd never had any, really.

"This Martha seems interesting, though. She sounds emotionally available, and she won't be leaving Australia any time soon," Amber said. "Two factors that can't be underestimated."

"I know, but we've only just met, and well, I can't get Robin out of my head." Today of all days, Micky wished Amber was the sort of person who brought over a bottle of wine instead of juice when she visited her best friend at home.

"That might be so, but I sense an opportunity here. Just for the record, I'm absolutely not suggesting you be dishonest with anyone, but I can see a possible happy ending here."

"Oh yeah?" Micky made no effort to keep the skepticism out of her voice.

"First of all, be upfront with both of them. You tell Robin you can't be friends with her, and you tell Martha you're still hung up on someone else but you're willing to go on a date with her. The worst that can happen is that you and Martha don't have that spark, but you stand to gain a genuine friend and learn from her along the way."

Though Amber's logic was, theoretically, irrefutable, she was missing the input of a large variable in her reasoning. "So, basically, what you're saying is 'Fuck Robin.'"

"I guess that is what I'm saying. She's not going to help you evolve, Micky. If anything, she'll stunt your growth as a person—as a lesbian. I know the sex was spectacular and all that, but that doesn't mean it can't be that way with anyone else. She was a good... *starter* woman for you. Made you realize a few things about yourself you were on the cusp of realizing anyway, but now you need to move on. Ultimately, she won't be able to give you what you want. We both know that. There's no use beating about the bush."

"That's easy for you to say." Micky felt like pouting.

"No, it's not easy for me to say at all. I'd much rather be telling you something you want to hear, but I wouldn't be a good friend if I did only that."

"I just don't know how to forget about Robin."

"It will take some time, most likely, but you need to tell her. Be honest. Tell her it's impossible for you to be friends with her because you'll always be hoping for more."

"Why must you be so logically gifted?"

Amber shrugged. "You know me, always better at giving advice to my friends than working on my own love life."

"How about, instead of going out with Martha on my own, I have a dinner party here next week, with you, Sheryl and Kristin, and her?"

"I guess that could work. I'm curious to meet Martha, and keen to spend some time with Sheryl and Kristin. They're so overwhelmingly nice."

"Do you also think there must be something hidden underneath that perfect exterior of theirs? Two people can't be *that* perfect together."

Amber broke out into a smile. "Oh, Micky." She shook her head.

"Come on," Micky insisted. "There must be something."

"We had dinner with them once. We don't know them that well."

Micky was enjoying the distraction of speculating about their acquaintances—who were turning into friends. "I wouldn't be surprised if Kristin moonlighted as a high-end

BDSM Mistress."

Amber narrowed her eyes, as though sunk deep into thought. "I could see that."

"Or maybe it's the other way around. You just never know."

"Sheryl? She's so laid-back... I don't know." Amber scrunched her lips together. "We only know one thing for sure. They are one hot couple."

"Shall I invite them then? I actually already spoke to Kristin about it."

"Sure. How about next Saturday, so I can let my hair down a bit?"

Micky chuckled. "I haven't seen you let your hair down in ten years."

"My version of it then. I'll drink two glasses of wine instead of one." Amber sat up a bit straighter. "Don't forget the task at hand. Why don't you text Robin now? And let Martha know about the dinner, ask her if she's free to join."

"Christ. Yes, boss." Micky looked her friend in the eyes for a fraction of a second. There was always nothing but good-heartedness to be found in them.

Micky did as she was told, inviting Martha to dinner first, then, her heart beating in her throat, sending a message to Robin saying: *I'm sorry, but I can't be friends with you. I would always be hoping for more.*

CHAPTER NINETEEN

It wasn't Micky's usual Sunday morning ritual to make French toast for her children, partly because Olivia had been listening to Amber's anti-sugar rants too much and only reluctantly pecked at her breakfast, and partly because Sunday morning breakfast was never a big deal.

It used to be, pre-divorce. Sunday was the only day of the week that Darren had focused all his attention on his family and he used to be the one to cook them eggs to order, with crispy bacon and bread he had fetched from the bakery on a brisk walk before any of them got up.

After Darren moved out, Micky had attempted to recreate the atmosphere of days past, but no matter how hard she tried, there would always be one person missing from their Sunday morning tableau. No amount of French toast could ever fill that gap.

But this particular Sunday morning, Micky was feeling especially guilty for robbing her children of a constant fatherly presence in their lives, and dipped white bread into a bowl of beaten eggs as though the very act could undo that knot in her stomach.

At the table where Olivia and Christopher were sitting now, a flock of lesbians would gather next week. And only seven short days ago—though it felt more like a lifetime— Micky had brought another woman into this house she shared with her children, and oh the things they had done. Micky straightened her posture and made sure the slice of bread she'd just transferred to the pan didn't stick. She didn't want to think of Robin right then. Preferably, she'd never think of Robin again, but her subconscious brain heartily disagreed. Although it did help that Robin had yet to reply to the message Micky sent the day before.

"Voilà." Micky presented Christopher with his breakfast first, hoping that the look of it would entice Olivia to have some as well. "French toast for my favorite man in the world."

"Thanks, Mom." He tucked in immediately, so when Micky asked what they wanted to do that day, his mouth was too full to reply.

"Can't we just hang out here? We don't have to do something every Sunday," Olivia said.

"What did you do last Sunday?" Micky asked casually.

"I told you already. Dad and Lisa took us to see a movie," Olivia said.

It was true that Micky already knew about this, but she wanted to find out more about Lisa. After all, her accompanying them to the movies was something entirely new to them—seeing their father with a woman who was not their mother.

Micky stopped the dipping of bread into egg and turned to face Olivia. "What's she like, then?" Micky had held in that particular question since she'd picked up the kids from school last Wednesday. She didn't want to be *that* kind of mother, but she was dying of curiosity.

"She's nice," Christopher said.

"He means she's hot." Olivia's lips were pursed together. They were at an age where they didn't seem to agree on anything. Olivia in particular made a point of challenging her brother every chance she got. Still, the comments about Lisa being *nice* and *hot* stung Micky on quite a few levels.

"No, I don't," Chris snarled.

"At least she doesn't have any children," Olivia said, doing what she did best: ignoring her brother.

Micky turned back to the stove and started frying more

toast. With her back to her children, her voice barely audible over the sizzle of the pan, she asked, "What was it like? Seeing your dad with someone else?"

"It wasn't too bad, as long as you're okay with it, Mom," Christopher said.

Olivia sighed, and said, "Why must you be *such* a suck-up?"

Micky could vividly imagine how she was rolling her eyes.

When Micky turned back around and presented Olivia with a plate of French toast, Chris held out his phone. "We took a photo at Gigi's after."

Micky took the phone in her hand and looked at the picture of her family, of her former life. Her space in the picture was taken up by a tiny woman who looked at least fifteen years younger than her.

"Oh, she's Asian," was all she said.

"Can you believe Lisa is thirty-nine, Mom?" Chris asked. There was a note of enthusiasm in his tone that Micky wasn't too fond of. "It's because she's Asian. They always look much younger than they actually are."

"That's so racist," Olivia started.

"What's racist about that?" Chris replied.

Micky let them bicker while she stared at the picture a little longer. Lisa looked perfectly nice. She had a very photogenic face—okay, she was *hot*. What caused the biggest twinge in Micky's stomach, though, was the fact that they'd all gone to Gigi's for ice cream after the movie. They always used to go there as a family. *Before.*

Micky put the phone down. She should be happy that Darren had met someone new, someone who her kids didn't immediately dislike. This was actually good news, she tried to convince herself.

"Mom, please explain to my idiot brother why what he just said about Lisa is racist." Olivia's voice was full of teenage indignation.

"Let it go, darling," Micky urged. She looked at her children, her beautiful boy and girl, and was overcome with a bout of nostalgia.

"How about you, Mom?" Chris asked. "Have you met someone else yet?" That snapped her right out of it.

Micky didn't believe in controlling anything physical with the mind, yet she hoped that how she was feverishly wishing not to break out into a telling blush would keep her from doing so.

"No. No, I haven't," she said quickly. In that moment, Micky knew she would have to tell her children sooner rather than later. Before she met someone and got serious about her. They were her children; they deserved to know. Yet Micky had no idea how to tell them. She was barely coming to grips with it herself. She would need to tell Darren first, which made her think about how he had inquired about her sexual preference with Amber. Perhaps it wouldn't come as a surprise to him, but it would to Liv and Chris.

"It was Mom who wanted her independence," Olivia said. Christ, the girl was on a roll this morning. At least she was eating.

When Micky and Darren had informed the children about their decision to divorce, they had told them what Micky then believed was nothing but the truth. Their mother and father had grown apart. They loved each other but weren't in love anymore—that old chestnut. It was better for everyone, the children included, if they didn't live in the same house anymore. Micky had tried to explain it in as gentle terms as possible and had tried to assure them that the pending divorce had nothing to do with them, that it was just a fact of life that, sometimes, it didn't work out between two people the way they had both hoped.

"It's not as if we didn't see it coming." Christopher was speaking for the both of them—Liv still kind of looked up to him back then.

It was the moment Micky had realized she was doing the right thing and that hurt her the most. She had always believed she and Darren had contained their differences, that their arguments couldn't be heard outside the closed door of their bedroom, but, of course, she realized then, children always know.

Micky didn't feel like getting into an argument with her daughter about this right then. Olivia was already on the war path this morning. It was high time for a change of subject, anyway. Micky needed to gather her thoughts, come up with a plan of action to tell her children eventually.

"How about I take you to the movies this afternoon?" she asked. "We'll go to Gigi's after."

✶ ✶ ✶

Micky had let the kids pick the movie, and it had been an unbelievably violent affair with supposed superheroes beating the crap out of everything. Perhaps she was getting too old for some things. Surprisingly, after they exited the theatre, Olivia's mood had brightened entirely, and she and Chris dissected the action parts of the movie with enthusiastic voices, agreeing on most things. This made Micky care less about the violent—and frankly ridiculous— nature of the film. She was just glad her teenagers were getting along for once.

When they arrived at the ice-cream parlor, while she was contemplating whether she could get away with ordering two scoops—it was Sunday after all—the first person she saw was Darren. Then her glance landed on the woman who was accompanying him. That picture Chris had shown her that morning didn't do her justice. It was as though some sort of force field radiated from her, the way her skin glowed and her eyes sparkled.

"Dad!" Olivia shouted when she clocked them.

"Hey, guys." Darren rose and threw his arms around Liv, then gave Chris a pat on the shoulder.

"Micky." He tensed when he approached Micky and

gave her a quick peck on the cheek. They weren't exactly estranged—just divorced. Still, Micky thought it was funny how things could go in life. Falling in love, getting married, and spending time on that fluffy cloud of love where everything seemed perfect. Having children and going through the subsequent trials and triumphs. Having a life so tied to another person's, you can't ever imagine not being with them. Until it's all you want. "What a surprise. Please, meet Lisa."

If she didn't know him better, she would have guessed Darren was gloating—but he really wasn't the type. He was probably feeling very uncomfortable about having to introduce his ex-wife to his new girlfriend in front of their children.

Lisa had already jumped out of her seat. God, the woman was tiny—petite but beautiful. Perhaps, once the day came that everything was out in the open and she and Darren had reached a space where they could just be friends again, they could compare women. "You picked a very striking one," Micky imagined herself saying. Inadvertently, she tried to gauge what Darren would think of Robin. The thought just popped into her head, even though it had no business being there. Robin still hadn't texted back, which was for the best. What did Micky expect? A big love declaration? *Yeah right.*

"So nice to meet you, Micky." She stretched out her hand. Micky thanked her lucky stars that she wasn't the hugging type. Micky shook Lisa's hand and was relieved to find it a bit clammy.

"Do you want to join us?" Darren asked.

"Sure." Micky could hardly say no. She might as well get this over with.

After they had all ordered their ice cream, sat huddled around a too small table, and had discussed the movies they had seen—the new Woody Allen for Darren and Lisa, though Micky couldn't for the life of her remember Darren ever saying a word about Woody Allen movies—the first awkward silence descended.

"So you work at Goodwin Stark," Micky said. Although it was a perfectly acceptable question, asking it had an unmistakable connection to Robin. Perhaps, if the children weren't there, she would have asked Lisa more about Goodwin Stark's glamorous new Diversity Manager, but now, she really couldn't.

"We actually kind of have the same job," Darren said. He looked into Lisa's eyes when he said it. Christ, he was smitten. As happy as she could rationally be for him, it was still odd to see her ex-husband mooning over another woman like this.

Lisa explained her job, which did sound a lot like Darren's, but if Micky was really being honest, she had lost track of Darren's career a decade ago. All she knew was that twelve-hour days were more normal than not, and that he was very handsomely paid for all the time he spent away from his family. Good for him that he'd found a girlfriend who worked the same hours as he did. And that the children were growing up fast. In fact, she pondered, Darren really was starting over. Something Micky had yet to accomplish. Though she did have a job now. And she'd had her first sexual encounter with a woman. Despite not having actually said the word out loud, not even to Amber, Micky knew she was a lesbian. At least she was no longer in denial about that. That was progress.

"How about you come to dinner at mine next Saturday, Micky?" Darren asked, seemingly out of the blue, though Micky had been zoned out of the conversation. "I could invite Josh and Charlotte. They've been asking after you."

Josh and Charlotte were the one couple they'd known since college that was still together. They hadn't been Micky and Darren's best friends as such, but there was a lingering sympathy and concern, and on and off, they had spent a lot of time together over the years.

"I'm sorry. I can't next Saturday," Micky said. "I'm throwing my own dinner party."

"Oh." Darren sounded a little deflated.

"Who's coming, Mom?" Olivia asked.

"Your auntie Amber. Kristin, my boss at The Pink Bean, and her wife Sheryl." Micky conveniently left out Martha. There was no point in telling them about her when they didn't know who she was.

He didn't say it out loud, but after what Amber had told her about Darren and the inquiry he had made about Micky, it was as though she could hear him think: *an all-ladies affair, huh?*

"How's Amber?" Darren asked instead.

"She's still single as well," Olivia said. Micky couldn't help but wonder what her daughter meant by that.

"Amber is doing just fine. She hopes to open her own yoga studio soon. She's going on a month-long retreat to India first, to *deepen her practice* as she puts it," Micky said.

"She's a yoga teacher?" Lisa asked.

Micky was surprised Olivia didn't treat her to a very ironic *Duh* at that obvious question. "Yes."

"Expert, more like," Darren said. "Amber doesn't do things halfheartedly. She's probably the best teacher in Sydney by now."

"I would love to try out one of her classes some time. My favorite teacher at my current studio left, and it just hasn't been the same since," Lisa said.

Lisa could want to do yoga all she wanted. She could even take Amber's classes, but Micky would make damn sure she didn't end up on the mat next to her tiny, probably ridiculously flexible body. She looked as though she could bend her legs all the way around her neck without exerting any effort.

"Darren has all the information," she said.

"Amber and I should talk. I've been looking for some alternative investment opportunities," Darren said.

He must have it really bad if Lisa got him to consider investing in a yoga studio. What was next? Doing yoga himself? Either way, Amber would never take Darren's money.

Micky just quirked up her eyebrows and gave him a quizzical look.

Then Lisa looked at her watch. "We'd best get going, babe," she said. "My parents are expecting us."

Upon hearing that Darren was already meeting Lisa's family, Micky concluded that, once you've reached a certain age, matters progressed much more swiftly—and she was lagging behind.

CHAPTER TWENTY

Amber had come over early to help Micky prepare for the dinner party. At least, that was what she called it. In Micky's eyes, it felt more like making sure enough vegetables and vegan-friendly dishes were served, even though Amber was the only vegan.

However, Amber's help was responsible for Micky being able to spend a little longer in the bathroom sprucing herself up before the other guests arrived. Working at The Pink Bean five days a week, and being on her feet for a couple of hours every day, had instigated a minor but not insignificant bout of weight loss, and Micky fit back into a dress she hadn't worn in ages but that had made the transfer from Mosman to Darlinghurst, because you just never knew. She was so pleased that her prediction about fitting into the dress again one day had been proven, that she descended the stairs with confidence, and when the bell rang and all three of the guests arrived at the same time, she let herself be pecked on the cheek and complimented about her looks unselfconsciously.

After introducing Martha to Amber and pouring everyone drinks, and reminding them that her cooking skills were more homely than culinary, Micky relaxed and raised her glass, content to be having this dinner at her new home. It was the first dinner party she had thrown since moving there, since leaving her old life behind. It was, though perhaps small in the grand scheme of things, a big event for her. A step in the right direction.

"Thank you all for coming," she said. She didn't add

that it felt like a fresh start for her to have a bunch of lesbians in her home, of which one was a potential love interest.

Martha was dressed casually in a linen blouse and jeans, which didn't stop her from looking good. She was probably one of those women who could throw on a rug and still look fabulous.

"To being here with you and not at my ex-husband and his new girlfriend's dinner party," she added, when they clinked the rims of their glasses together.

"Don't tell me," Martha said, "she's at least ten years younger than him."

"Don't be so bitter." Sheryl patted her colleague on the shoulder. "Trevor did you a favor in the end."

"If you want to call it that." Martha sipped from her wine. "Anyway, let's not talk about our ex-husbands tonight. Surely we have far more interesting topics to discuss." She let her glance rest on Micky for an instant, as though insinuating that Micky was one of those topics.

Micky smiled at her sheepishly. This was the first time she had seen Martha again since they'd met. She hadn't had a chance to discuss with her what Amber had implored her to do. Not that Micky saw much point to that now. Robin hadn't been to The Pink Bean once this week, nor had she texted back. Micky might as well remove her number from her phone. An act she had considered doing—for ritual cleansing purposes—that morning, because whenever she closed her eyes, or just before opening them, all she still saw was Robin all over her. When she focused really hard, she could conjure up her smell. And she had no trouble recalling how the grip of Robin's fingers around her wrist felt. But that was over now. In the past. Time to look ahead. Which was, at this very moment, straight into Martha's kind eyes.

It wasn't as though, when she allowed herself to, Micky couldn't see herself together with a woman like Martha. Mere weeks ago, it was all she ever dreamed of. But that was before Robin had showed her how easily initial attraction can turn into unbearable lust and… this yearning that Micky just couldn't shake. A tiny part of her, even as she sat there feeling pretty pleased with herself surrounded by these women in her home, wished this was a dinner party to introduce Robin to the group.

But it wasn't. So she'd better get a grip.

"How about I bring out some snacks?" Amber said.

Only a few minutes into the evening and Micky was already neglecting her hostess duties. She really needed to pull it together and erase all memories of that Saturday night of two weeks ago from her brain.

"I'll help you," Martha volunteered, and they headed into the open kitchen.

"How have you been, Micky?" Sheryl asked. "Kristin tells me you lost her a loyal customer?" It was clearly meant as a joke, but it still nagged at Micky.

"Leave her alone, Sheryl," Kristin said. "At least now we don't have to make wet cappuccinos anymore."

Just the day before, Kristin had brought up Robin. Micky had just finished her shift and was packing up to leave the coffee shop when Kristin had said, "She really does seem to have moved on, from both of us." She'd bumped her shoulder into Micky's and continued, "But not to worry, a certain professor is very excited about seeing you again tomorrow."

It had struck Micky then how quickly she had gone from being in denial to being attracted to one woman while another was attracted to her. Perhaps it was the effect Robin had had on her that was rubbing off on her and making her look interesting to Martha. Something with pheromones and whatnot. She'd made a mental note to google that, but hadn't gotten around to it. Either way, all this week, and even still that night, there had only been one conclusion to every thought she'd had: Robin and how that was now dead in the water.

"It's a good thing," Amber had said when she'd arrived earlier. "It's best not to wear these things out too long."

"Here we go," Amber said and presented Kristin and Sheryl with a tray of hummus and aubergine dip she had brought.

✶ ✶ ✶

"What with it being all the rage these days, I've tried it several times, but I could just never get the hang of it. I'm sure it's me, but I don't have the right mindset to practice yoga," Martha said to Amber after learning she was an instructor.

Uh-oh, here we go. That's the conversation hijacked for the next thirty minutes. Mickey loved Amber dearly, but she could go on and on about a subject she was passionate about. Yoga was number one on her list.

"Then I can only assume you just haven't come across the right instructor for you yet," Amber, to Micky's great surprise, simply said. "I invite you to come to one of my classes and I will happily change your mind."

Martha smiled at her, then cocked her head. "Such utter confidence. I like it."

Amber smiled back with the most wattage her smile could muster, then looked away from Martha, stared briefly at Micky, and folded her features into a more demure expression again.

"Can you give me a quick hand in the kitchen, please?" Micky asked.

"Sure." Amber jumped up promptly.

Micky ushered her into the utility room. "What do you think of Martha?" she asked.

"She is really nice. So interesting, well-spoken, and frankly, gorgeous. I say go for it!" Her voice shot up.

"I thought you would say that." Micky tried to hold Amber's gaze, but her glance kept flitting away.

"What do you mean?"

"Instead of giving her the yoga speech, you just invited

her to one of your classes." Micky couldn't keep a note of indignation from her voice.

"So?"

"In all the years you've discovered yoga, I've never known you to not give the speech."

"What are you insinuating?" Amber asked.

Micky took a breath. "You like her."

"No, I don't." There was no conviction to Amber's words. She was incapable of lying, especially to Micky.

"You were just summing up all her good qualities."

"For you, just to tip you over the edge. She likes you, any fool can see that."

A knock on the door startled them. "Everything okay in here?" Kristin asked. "You probably didn't hear, Micky, but your doorbell just rang. Has the stripper arrived early?" she joked.

"What?" Instantly, Micky thought about the children. Where was her phone? Had Darren tried to reach her?

"Do you want me to get it?" Kristin asked.

"I'll get it," Amber offered. She was probably in a panic as well—or happy to not be subjected to Micky's questions any longer. She scooted out of the tiny utility room where they had been cramped together.

Micky had completely forgotten why she had come into the kitchen in the first place, apart from wanting to quiz Amber.

"Micky." Amber stuck her head into the kitchen. "You may want to come out here."

"What is it?"

Amber looked more amused than anything else.

With a thudding heart, Micky made her way to the hallway, only to find Robin standing in her doorway.

"I'll leave you to it," Amber said, and ducked past Micky, back into the living room.

Apart from a closed-off washroom, the ground floor of Micky's house was one big space, and the only separation

155

between the hallway and the living room, where her guests were gathered, and probably wondering what was going on, was a small dividing wall with no door.

"I'm sorry," Robin said. "You have guests. I should have called or texted." Just then, a cloud broke, and rain started pelting down on the sidewalk.

Micky didn't know what to say or do, so she just pulled Robin inside and closed the door behind her.

What was she doing there?

★ ★ ★

"I'm having some people over," Micky said after the first shock of Robin turning up out of the blue had subsided. "Do you want to join us? You can hardly go out in that rainstorm."

"I don't want to intrude, Micky. I just wanted to say something... in private. But I guess that's out of the question." She took a step backward toward the door. "I'll come back some other time."

"Don't be silly." Micky had no idea what she was doing. She wanted to hear what Robin wanted to say so badly.

"Look," Robin whispered. "I get that you don't want to be just friends. Turns out I'm not so keen on the idea either, what with not being able to stop thinking about you."

Micky's eyes grew wide. Had she heard that correctly? Had Robin just said, in hushed and conspiratorial tones, exactly what she had wanted to hear?

"That's all I wanted to say. Why don't you give me a call tomorrow?" Robin made for the door again. "You'd better get back to your guests." She cast one last glance at Micky, opened the door, and disappeared into the pouring rain.

Micky just stood there for a while longer, savoring the moment, though it had already passed. Goodness. Robin wanted to be more than friends. Damn. Martha was sitting in her living room. And Amber... she would have to come to her rescue once again. She'd have to come down from her moral high ground and turn up the flirting with Martha. It wasn't as if she hadn't already been doing it anyway.

Micky stepped back into the living room to find all four of them staring at her. Micky hadn't told Martha about Robin. What was she supposed to say?

"Sorry about the interruption." She headed to the kitchen. Which course were they at again? Oh yes, she'd served the mains and it was almost time for dessert. Underneath the panic about the food and keeping her company entertained, however, Micky was in full rejoice mode. Robin's words were starting to really sink in. She wanted nothing more than to run after her, tell her how she felt—although she guessed she'd made that clear already.

She rummaged around in the kitchen for a couple of minutes, doing nothing in particular while she tried to gather her thoughts. Right. Dessert. Micky hadn't made a big deal out of it and had just bought five tartlets at the most upmarket bakery she knew. In her experience, once guests reached dessert, they were either too full from the copious previous dishes, or too boozed up to truly enjoy her efforts.

She turned away from the sink and the stack of dirty dishes inside it. "Coffee anyone?"

"Why don't you come sit with us for a bit and have something stronger," Sheryl said. "You look like you need it."

Micky was so happy Sheryl was there. If it had just been Amber, she'd be boiling water for a cup of peppermint tea—because green tea this late at night was not a good idea according to Amber.

"I know where she keeps the good stuff." Amber got up and headed for the drinks cabinet.

"Do you want to talk about it?" Sheryl asked. "Or am I being too nosy?"

Micky sat down. She had put herself across from Martha, whom she couldn't look in the face right then.

"Don't worry about me, Micky," Martha said. "Sheryl briefed me about Robin. She wouldn't have been a very good friend if she hadn't."

"I'm sorry. I thought it was over," Micky said. This was a very odd thing to be apologizing for, especially because Micky felt more like jumping up and down with glee.

Amber deposited five glasses and an unopened bottle of brandy on the table.

"This is good news," Kristin added.

"It is. It's just a bit unexpected, and well, the timing is a bit off, I guess." Micky couldn't help a stupid grin from appearing on her face.

"What are you going to do?" Sheryl asked.

Have really amazing sex and probably have my heart broken. "I'll go see her tomorrow."

Amber planted a, by her measures, generously filled glass of brandy in front of Micky.

"I guess we'll just be friends then." Martha held up her glass for an impromptu toast.

Micky could kiss her, though that would be a bit ironic, for sucking some tension from the room like that.

She was finally able to hold Martha's gaze for longer than a split second. "I would really like that."

Next to her, though she would never admit it, Amber sat beaming.

CHAPTER TWENTY-ONE

Micky desperately wanted to get some sleep, but it was impossible. She'd also been a bit too liberal with the brandy in order to calm her nerves. She lay tossing and turning in her bed, alone, thinking that she could be in Robin's bed right then. "Patience," she kept whispering to herself, as she calculated what would be a decent time to call Robin the next morning.

Oh, screw it. She could just send a message now. She'd waited long enough.

Can't sleep, she typed. *Can't wait to see you tomorrow.*

She hoped that at least giving Robin a sign that she was very appreciative of her gesture would give her some peace of mind. It didn't. She also didn't want to fall asleep now in case Robin was suffering from insomnia as well. She lay on her side, glancing at her phone on the nightstand, waiting for it to light up with a message.

While she did, she considered how graciously Martha had taken Robin's interruption. Micky didn't feel too guilty about that, though, because the spark between her and Amber had been so obvious. After everyone had left, Micky had teased Amber about it, and her friend had turned beet red—to Micky's great delight.

Just as she started dozing off, sheer exhaustion taking over, her phone lit up. Instantly, Micky was wide awake again.

Can't sleep either. Shall I come over?

Oh God. *Yes, please*, was Micky's first thought, but her house was a mess after the dinner party, dishes piled high in the open kitchen—not to mention how messy Micky herself looked. Additionally, the rainstorm that had started when Robin rang her bell had softened a little, but it was still pouring down outside. Micky couldn't, in good conscience, ask Robin to make her way to her through that kind of weather again.

I'll come to you, she texted back.

She jumped out of bed and was reminded that she was operating on no sleep at all. But, to hell with it, she could still pull an all-nighter. As soon as she got to Robin's, she could sink into her embrace, and fall into the most blissful sleep. *Yeah, right.*

Micky took a quick shower, but did nothing to her hair because the rain would ruin it, anyway. Then she set off into the dark, stormy night. Just walking out of her door at two in the morning was a thrill—and then there was the woman she was going to see.

✴ ✴ ✴

As soon as Micky rang the bell, Robin's intercom buzzed. She must have been lying in wait. Micky stabbed the elevator button frantically, then when it didn't arrive soon enough, decided to take the stairs instead.

With energy she had no idea she possessed, she rushed up the stairs to Robin's place. The door was ajar when she got there.

Out of breath, but her entire being pulsing with adrenaline, Micky slowly pushed the door open.

Robin stood in the middle of the living room, wearing only a pair of stripy boy shorts and a very tight tank top.

The adrenaline in Micky's body quickly turned into something fierier, more urgent. Without saying a word, she shoved the door shut behind her, not breaking eye contact with Robin, and took a few quick strides toward her.

Micky's jacket—she hadn't even had the presence of mind to take an umbrella—was dripping raindrops onto the floor. It was the only sound, apart from her quickening breath, in the apartment.

"There you are," Robin said, and bridged the remaining gap between them.

She unzipped Micky's rain jacket and just let it fall to the floor, into the small puddle it had already created.

First and foremost, Micky was overcome with lust, but it wasn't the only emotion throbbing underneath her skin. There was relief and gratitude and something else she couldn't quite put her finger on just yet. It didn't matter. She was there.

Robin folded her strong arms around Micky. "I know we need to talk, but can we do that tomorrow?" she whispered into Micky's ear.

Micky nodded, her chin bumping against Robin's shoulder. Oh, those shoulders and how her shoulder line looked in that tank top. Micky was beginning to salivate. She pressed her lips against Robin's skin and inhaled her scent.

She felt Robin's hands tugging at her T-shirt, starting to hoist it up. "I want you," Robin whispered, and Micky thought she might crash to her knees.

Not as much as I want you, Micky wanted to say, but she was just glad to hear the words. They would deal with the consequences of their desire later. Now, it was the middle of the night, and they had a lot of unfinished business to attend to.

Robin pulled Micky's T-shirt over her head, then unsnapped her jeans button.

That's right. Why waste time? In the short time span she'd been in Robin's apartment and in her magnetic presence, her entire being had turned into red hot desire, into fast-breathing lust. All she wanted was Robin all over her again. It was all she had wanted since Robin left her house that Sunday.

Robin pushed Micky's jeans down while Micky tried to kick off her shoes. They were wet and stuck to her feet, but she managed in the end, and then she stood in front of Robin in just her underwear. No matter how flimsy—Micky had dressed for the occasion—it still felt like too much on her, too much fabric covering crucial parts of her.

"Come here." Robin pulled her to her and then, at last, kissed her.

While their lips met, brazen and wide from the get-go, Robin's hands were all over Micky's body, and Micky wasn't shy herself. She pressed her fingertips into Robin's strong biceps, let herself get carried away by the firmness of her body, not caring one bit about how her own looked in comparison. Because Robin had come to her, had chosen her.

While their lips remained glued together, and their tongues danced with each other, Robin spun Micky around and walked her backward until her back touched the wall.

Robin quickly proceeded, while keeping her lips glued to Micky's, to bring her hands between Micky's back and the wall to unsnap her bra. This made Micky wonder about the point of bothering to wear sexy lingerie if it was going to come off so swiftly—a course of action she very much agreed with. Besides, Robin's shorts and tank top were so much hotter, although, again, Micky just wanted to rip them off her. So she did.

Their lips broke apart, and Micky reached for Robin's top. Robin lifted up her arms, and Micky pulled it over her head, not as smoothly as she would have wanted to, because the garment was tight and its fabric not very stretchy. But then, Robin's glorious breasts were unveiled to her once again. Micky felt her panties go even damper. Before Robin, Micky had gone without the sensual touch of another human being for years, and look at what the effect of two weeks without Robin was having on her now. Her clit was pounding, her nipples were rock hard, her entire body was aching to be covered by all of Robin.

"Turn around," Robin whispered.

Micky cocked her head, not quite sure what Robin

meant. Besides, if she faced the wall, she wouldn't have her eyes on Robin's chest anymore, and where was the fun in that?

"Go on." Robin put her hands on Micky's waist and coaxed her until Micky swiveled around. Micky had to be honest with herself. If Robin asked her to fly to the moon right then, she probably would—as long as the reward was Robin's fingers buried deep in her pussy afterward.

Micky planted her hands against the wall and, as soon as she felt Robin's hands on her back, closed her eyes. Robin's fingers trailed down the skin of her back, along the waistband of her panties, which must be fully drenched by now. Robin hooked a finger underneath and, slowly, pulled the panties down Micky's behind and legs. Micky stepped out of them, and finally, she was freed of all constraints. She spread her legs and took a deep breath. She was more than ready for whatever Robin had in store for her. Admittedly, not being able to see what Robin was doing, or being able to gauge her next move, was arousing.

A trickle of wetness escaped from Micky's nether lips. This must be the wettest she'd ever been in her life. Now Robin pressed her firm breasts against Micky's back and her lips touched down on her neck, then her right shoulder. Meanwhile, Robin's hands fluttered down her sides, over her belly, skimmed along her pubic hair.

"I couldn't stop thinking about you," Robin whispered in her ear, then she let her teeth sink into Micky's earlobe. "The more I tried to ignore your existence, the more I wanted you."

To Micky, hearing these words had the same effect as having two fingers slipped inside her wet and wanting pussy. Robin's fingertips skirting her skin and her lips hovering around her ear and neck felt like tiny shocks of electricity being administered. A sensation Micky wanted more of, though there was something else she wanted even more. Then, completely free of inhibitions and whatever logic, faulty or otherwise, had stopped her from doing so, Micky spoke the words that were at the forefront of her mind.

"Fuck me," she said. "Oh, please, fuck me."

Robin gave a breathy chuckle in her ear. "Oh, I will, Micky. I will." Her hands meandered along Micky's back, to her buttocks, where they traced along Micky's skin in the lightest of touches.

More juices slid down Micky's inner thighs. She'd be creating a puddle on the floor soon, like her wet jacket had done earlier. Extreme wetness really was the theme of this night.

Robin's fingers had reached Micky's inner thighs now. They trailed upward, and Micky braced herself, but the fingers kept caressing instead of going where Micky so desperately wanted them. In that moment, it felt like she had been waiting for Robin's fingers to enter her for as long as she could remember. She was done waiting. She turned around, pushing Robin away from her in the process, grabbed her by the wrist, and pulled her close again.

"Please," she begged. "I need you now."

Robin's glance went soft. She brought her face so close to Micky's, their noses almost touched. She shook her hand free from Micky's grasp and, without taking her eyes off Micky, brought her hand where Micky had wanted it all along—or at least for the past two weeks, which seemed to have been condensed into this moment.

This time, when Micky braced herself, Robin's fingers did enter. Slowly, stretching Micky wide. She was filled with Robin. Her dream was coming true.

Micky brought one hand to the back of Robin's head and the other to one of her breasts. This was beyond any dreams she'd dared to have. Was this even really happening? But, oh, yes, Robin's fingers delved a little deeper, and her blue eyes were still gazing at Micky.

Micky's breath was already faltering, stopping and starting in short gusts. Robin's fingers inside of her were really all she needed ever again. And the feel of her breast in her hand. And those beautiful eyes on her.

Robin's serious expression changed into a slight smile —one that said she knew exactly what she was doing *and* what Micky wanted. To have a woman like Robin doing this to her. No matter how nice Martha was and how much they had in common, Micky had, on some level, known it would never work unless she'd had a few months to get over Robin first. Because Robin did something to her. This wasn't just the effect the first woman she'd ever slept with was having on her. This was Robin. The combination of them together.

Robin's fingers found a spot inside of her that seemed to make all of Micky's thoughts come to an abrupt halt. All the desire she'd kept bottled up for the past two weeks came crashing through her flesh, pooled between her legs, clamped itself around Robin's fingers.

And if Micky had one thought flitting through her mind in that moment when Robin fucked her so deliciously, so knowingly, as though it was all she'd ever done in her life, it was that this wasn't just an orgasm, it was a reunion. There was no way that, after this, Micky wouldn't let her feelings be known down to the tiniest detail.

"Oh God," she moaned, holding on to the wall for support, while the heat spread through her flesh.

When Micky's eyes fluttered open, she was greeted by Robin's wide smile.

"Worth a midnight trip through the pouring rain?" Robin asked.

The climax seemed to have taken the last of Micky's energy. She just nodded, mirroring Robin's smile.

"Come to bed with me," Robin said. "I presume you're sleeping over."

CHAPTER TWENTY-TWO

When Micky woke up, she was alone in bed. She looked for the alarm clock. It was ten thirty-two. She sank back into the pillows, perking up her ears for a sign of Robin, but all was quiet.

What a night she'd had. The dinner party, followed by Robin ringing her bell, and then coming over here. She thought about Amber and Martha. And about what Kristin and Sheryl must think of her now. And whether Darren would be shocked if he found out. And about Christopher and Olivia, who now had a mother who fled the house in the middle of the night to have sex with another woman. All the conversations she still needed to have. But then her mind drifted back to Robin, to her blue eyes and the smile on her face and how, with the lightest touch of her finger, she could make Micky go all liquid inside.

Micky hadn't fallen in love since Darren. She'd all but forgotten what it felt like. She remembered now. Michaela Ferro had gone and fallen head-over-heels in love with another woman. And, by the look of things, Robin was headed in the same direction.

She heard the front door fall into the lock. Some stumbling in the living room. Then Robin came into the bedroom, her hair wet, her skin scrubbed clean, with a Pink Bean carrying tray containing two cups. "You're up. Great," she said. "I thought you might like this."

Micky chuckled. "I can't believe you went to The Pink Bean."

"Where else am I going to go?" She sat down on the

bed and handed Micky a cup. "You didn't stir one bit this morning. At one point, I actually put my hand on your chest to check if your heart was still beating."

"You exhausted me."

"It must have been all that cooking you did beforehand." Robin scooted a little closer. "I'm so sorry for crashing your party."

"You do, indeed, look extremely apologetic." A rush of happiness shot up Micky's spine. She could easily imagine waking up like this every Sunday. Well, every other Sunday, perhaps.

"I did my very best to express exactly how sorry I was last night. Wouldn't you agree?" Robin wiggled her eyebrows.

"Wholeheartedly." Micky broke out into a smile. "Thank you for coming over like that. Truth be told, I couldn't stop thinking about you either."

"Oh, is that why you had a bunch of lesbians at your house last night?" Robin blew cold air onto the froth of her cappuccino.

"What else was I going to do?" Micky put her coffee, which was still too hot to drink, on the nightstand next to her and shuffled closer to Robin.

"You could have waited for me to show up at your door in heartbreaking solitude." Robin disposed of her cup as well.

"And you could have texted me back." Micky sat close enough to Robin to inhale her freshly showered scent.

"You were the one who told me you'd met someone, remember?" Robin fixed her with a stare.

"I did meet someone. She was at my house last night. But all I could think of was you."

"Poor woman," Robin said, "though I don't feel *that* sorry for her."

"I think Amber will be there to pick up the pieces."

"Really?" Robin tipped her head and leaned in a little closer.

"I'll tell you all about it later." Micky kissed her on the cheek, then fully on the lips. They had all day to talk—and kiss, and make love.

★ ★ ★

Later, over a late lunch of pizza and wine in the middle of the afternoon, Micky couldn't stop gazing into Robin's eyes. They had a lot of things to talk about, but Micky was content just sitting there with Robin, and having the pleasure of being able to look at her as much as she wanted. There was one question burning in her mind, though. Not one she had any right to ask, but she was dying to know the answer to.

She cleared her throat, drank some wine, then spoke. "Did you, er, sleep with anyone else in the past two weeks?"

Robin drew her lips into a grin. "Why do you ask?"

"Well, you know, you *don't do* relationships and such, and… you must get propositioned a lot."

"Propositioned?" Robin huffed out a chuckle. "Do you get propositioned a lot?"

"Well, I don't mean to brag but…" She sank her teeth into her bottom lip.

"I didn't sleep with anyone else, Micky." Robin's voice was suddenly low and serious. "I told you. I couldn't stop thinking about you. And then you told me about this other woman, which was a genius move, by the way."

"You were jealous." Micky's eyes widened.

Robin cocked her head. "I was." She transferred a slice of pizza from the serving dish to her plate. "That day you took me to the beach, I had such an amazing time. I don't just mean us sleeping together afterward. I mean the entire weekend. I only realized it too late. We have a ton of chemistry between us, that's for sure, but I also just like being with you. Just sitting here with you, talking, getting to know you better. I want to know everything about you, in fact."

"But, er, isn't that against your… policy?"

"I wouldn't call it a policy. It's more me trying to rely on common sense. I have no business falling for someone when there's no future for us, but you know, the heart wants what the heart wants. Last night, I was sitting at home, feeling very sorry for myself. The classic image of a woman by herself gazing out of the window, watching the clouds gather before the storm rolls in, with a half-empty bottle of wine by my side. This life I lead, it can get very lonely. Moving from city to city, starting over again every two years, building a social life from scratch. Which is why I asked to go back to the US after my stint in Sydney. I've had enough of this life. This last year away from home was going to be my craziest one. I mean, this is Sydney. Diversity will always need to be promoted anywhere in the world, at least for a good long while to come, but this isn't Asia. Spending a year here is basically a working sabbatical for me. I have work to do, for sure, but it's not as strenuous and frustrating as what I was trying to accomplish in Hong Kong and Singapore. And I had one rule only: have as much fun as possible and don't fall in love." She paused, picked up the slice of pizza, then put it back. "My plan was working pretty well. Then I met you."

Micky's pulse picked up speed. Her mind focused on the very last sentence Robin had spoken, from which Micky deduced that Robin was falling in love with her as well. This, however, didn't change anything about their situation in the long run. Robin would still be leaving at the end of the year. But it was only March. There were nine more months in the year. Perhaps Robin could take some time off after. At this point, everything was still possible. Micky had no other choice but to believe that.

"I wish I could say I was sorry, but I'm really not," Micky said.

Robin smiled, but only briefly. "What I did last night, running over to your house in a frenzy like that, was surely impulsive. That was me not abiding by common sense at all.

But I don't regret it in the slightest. I was overcome by this urge to see you, to tell you that I didn't just want to be friends either, with benefits or not. I want more. I want to date you. It might have been foolish, but I couldn't stop myself."

"Then let's date," Micky said. "Let's be foolish and date."

Robin bent over the table. "On the sly, you mean? I can't leave my panties lying around at your house, I presume?"

Micky chuckled nervously. "I know you lesbians are very quick about these things and all that, but we've only just met, so let's hold off on the U-Haul for now."

"Good lord, don't tell me you just made a U-Haul joke." Robin banged her hands on the table. "Not even out of the closet yet, but already making the joke."

Micky glanced at Robin, trying to figure out if, somewhere during this line of banter, she had become serious about the matter, or if she was just teasing Micky for being a forty-four-year-old woman in the closet.

Robin sat smiling, picked up the slice of pizza again, and finally took a bite.

"I met my ex-husband's new partner the other weekend. I was at the cinema with the kids and we ran into them."

"Oh yes, Lisa, right? I happen to have met a Lisa at work this week." She wiggled her eyebrows.

"What?" Micky asked, though she knew very well what Robin was getting at.

"P.Y.T.," Robin said.

"What?" Now Micky really was confused.

"Pretty young thing? Michael Jackson song? No?" Robin gave her an amused expression. "But don't worry, Micky, she's actually older than me. I looked her up on the company's intraweb. We can double-date some time, if you like."

"I should probably tell Darren about this… us."

"You tell him when you're ready. How long was he seeing Lisa before he told you?"

"A few weeks. But that's different."

"Why is it different?"

"Because… Darren isn't seeing another man all of a sudden. If it had been the case, and he was bringing a guy into the house where my children spend half of their time, I'd want to know as quickly as possible."

"Why is it so different?"

"Because their father would suddenly be gay and I imagine we would need to have a conversation about how to tell the kids."

"Why would you need to be involved in telling your kids their father is gay? And why are we talking about this as though your ex is the one who's gay? It's got nothing to do with him."

"They're his children, too."

"Yes, of course they are, but you're the one who's dating a woman. I agree that, once you're ready, you should inform him about your decision to tell the kids, just as he did you the same courtesy, but that's where it ends. His further opinion doesn't matter, because it's your life."

Micky swallowed a big gulp of wine. "How old were you when you came out?" She made a mental note to get in touch with Martha. Not only because she could have been more upfront with her and she should, perhaps, apologize for not telling her about her lingering feelings for Robin, but because collecting coming-out stories suddenly seemed like a necessity before she could do her own.

"I was twenty-five when I told my parents." Robin fell silent.

Micky had expected her to have much more to say about the subject. "And?"

Robin sighed. "I'd like to think they've fully accepted it by now, but a part of me thinks they never will. Not that they would ever tell me so, but it's just a feeling I get. I can try to explain to them that it's nobody's fault and so on and so forth until the cows come home, but I know that no rational explanation will ever change how they feel deep inside. The sort of life I lead..." Robin shook her head. "It's so far removed from how they've been brought up and lived theirs. Not just my choice in partners, but being an expat. Everything. They're good people, but the distance between us just seems to get bigger and bigger, and I don't just mean the physical distance."

"I wasn't expecting that," Micky said.

"Because I travel around coaxing people out of the closet and pushing them to stand up for their rights?" Robin started playing with her unused fork. "Which is a gross oversimplification of what I do, by the way. Discrimination toward minorities is so terribly ingrained in every culture and society I've ever come across. Even my own parents, you know? They're hardly hillbillies, not by a long shot, yet I've always gotten the impression that, despite really doing their best, they just can't fully grasp the difference between us. But that's just the thing: why would I be different from them? I'm not. Not really. I'm as much their child as my brother is, except that I haven't followed the path they'd dreamed up for me since the moment they knew they were pregnant with me. Instead I veered so off course, I'm just a dot in the distance to them now, I sometimes think." Robin's gaze drifted to somewhere behind Micky.

"Is that why you do what you do?" Micky asked.

"I do what I do because I can't stand it when people get treated differently just for being who they are. It makes my blood boil." Robin expelled a sigh again. "I'm sorry, Micky. I didn't mean to get all heavy on you. In general, I am accepted, even respected for what I do and who I am. I'm one of the lucky ones, really." A forced smile appeared on her face. "And I think you will be too. If anything, you have Amber, whom I would love to get to know better, for the record. You have your job at The Pink Bean. You have children who were raised open-mindedly in this day and age. As daunting as the road ahead seems, I have a sneaking suspicion you will be all right."

"Do you give a lot of inspirational speeches?" Micky wanted to lighten the tone.

"I've given a few in my day." The subsequent smile on Robin's face seemed more spontaneous.

"I can tell." Micky responded to Robin's smile in kind. "I would very much like for you and Amber to get to know each other better." Micky proceeded to tell Robin about her and Amber's near-life-long friendship, then said, "Maybe we'll be double-dating with her and Martha soon."

CHAPTER TWENTY-THREE

Nerves rattled Micky's stomach, even though of all the gatherings she was yet to have in the weeks to come, this one should be the least nerve-racking. Kristin had organized an open mic poetry night at The Pink Bean, and she and Robin were going together. It was a Friday evening, and her kids were home alone, a fact for which Micky felt disproportionally guilty, despite Liv and Chris being old enough to stay at the house alone and take care of themselves.

"I'm going to an event at The Pink Bean," Micky had said.

"Wow, you really can't stay away from that place, Mom," Olivia had replied. "When can I try the coffee?"

Micky could only hope her daughter hadn't seen the flyer for the open mic tonight, which had been very much advertised as LGBT-focused.

Amber, Kristin, and Sheryl would be there—perhaps even Martha—and Micky was eager to introduce Robin to them officially. But it was all so new and so different from anything else she'd ever done. Micky might be forty-four, but she'd only had one significant relationship in her life so far. Up until her divorce, she had probably followed the exact path her parents had dreamed up for her. While still at university, she'd fallen in love with a man no parent would disapprove of, quickly followed up by marrying and having a boy and a girl—how perfect was that? Micky had followed all the rules, had done exactly what everyone had always expected of her. She even had a lesbian best friend, for added political correctness.

One life event had flowed into the next, and she'd never had to stop to think about whether any of the things she did were socially acceptable or frowned upon. Walking to The Pink Bean that night was an entirely different experience, because, to her, it felt as though she was breaking every rule possible and, more disconcertingly, she didn't really know how to behave. She had a lot of questions rummaging in the back of her mind. On top of all that, this was also Micky's first official LGBT activity. It wasn't a coming out as such, but she would at least be considered by many as gay by association.

When she arrived at the coffeehouse, Robin was already there. She was chatting to a woman Micky didn't recognize.

Robin kissed her on the lips, then introduced her to the woman. "This is Meredith, a colleague who got extremely excited when I told her about tonight's poetry night."

Micky shook hands with Meredith, hoping she wasn't the chatty type at the office, and didn't work with Lisa. This was all too close for comfort. She would need to tell Darren sooner rather than later.

Amber arrived. Micky hadn't seen or spoken to her all week because she'd gone on a five-day yoga retreat in Queensland where cell phones and the internet were not allowed. "It's not just a physical detox," Amber had said, "but also a digital one." Micky had missed her best friend so much, she wanted to hug her and linger in Amber's comforting embrace for a good long while. They all said hello, and even before Micky had the time to inquire with Amber whether she'd been in touch with Martha at all, Kristin tapped the microphone and called for everyone's attention.

★ ★ ★

"Honestly," Micky whispered in Robin's ear, "I'm not really one for poetry, but your colleague was very good. She was my favorite."

"I'll recite some for you later," Robin replied.

They applauded Meredith and watched her walk back to her seat. Then Kristin took back the mic and thanked everyone for coming. The Pink Bean was not licensed to serve alcohol, so not many audience members were inclined to stick around on a Friday night.

"I'm meeting my friends in a bar in Newtown," Meredith said. "Do you guys want to join?"

"I'm sorry, but I can't," Micky said.

"I'll hang out here with Micky," Robin said.

After Meredith had left, Robin said, "Have you ever been to Newtown? It's where all the lesbians hang out."

Micky just chuckled and shook her head. "She's not going to, er, tell anyone at work about me, is she?" Sydney was a big city, but the banking world was small, and not a lot of bankers' ex-wives went by the nickname Micky.

"About the hot piece of ass I'm dating? How can you possibly expect her to be discreet about that?" Robin joked and kissed her on the cheek.

Micky hadn't seen Robin since saying good-bye to her quickly on Wednesday morning. Robin had been leading a two-day workshop on a subject matter Micky had forgotten about and hadn't come into The Pink Bean for her daily coffee. Micky had thought about her every single second.

After most of the small crowd had dispersed, Micky found herself huddled around a table with Robin, Amber, and Sheryl, while Kristin and Alyssa cleared up. Micky had offered to help, but Kristin had waved her off, claiming it would be done in no time as she winked at Micky ostentatiously.

"While you're here," Sheryl said to Robin, "can you make this country a little less backward and tell the government they're utter pillocks for not having passed marriage equality yet? It's just ludicrous."

"I'll do my best, but I have to say, I never thought the

US would legalize it in all states before Australia did. It is, indeed, ludicrous."

"Would you and Kristin get married?" Amber asked.

"At this point, I truly don't know." Sheryl slanted her body over the table. "Kristin asked me to marry her when New Zealand legalized it, but I had to say no. Just out of sheer principle. What's the point of getting married somewhere else, only to return to a country that doesn't recognize it? We have all our paperwork in order, anyway. I know she asked me for romantic purposes, because why else bother? But, Goddamn it, it's just so unfair, and I'm so sick of being treated like a second-class citizen and not having the same rights as all those heterosexual people who get married without giving it a second thought, then end up divorced and bitter ten years later." She shook her head. "No offense, Micky," she added.

"None taken, but I guess you're right." Truth be told, Micky hadn't given the whole marriage equality issue a lot of thought. She'd been married. She wasn't planning on doing that again. She couldn't possibly see the point of once more promising herself to one person for the rest of her life. She'd been there, done that, and had the emotional scars to show for it.

"Hey, Amber, Martha's been asking about you," Sheryl said next. Clearly she'd spent the better part of the poetry readings finishing her own personal bottle of wine—despite The Pink Bean's lack of license. "Now that Micky here"— she pointed her thumb at Micky—"is off the table." She followed up with a deep-bellied chuckle. "But it's okay, we're all lesbians, after all."

Micky didn't see what was so funny about that, although Sheryl obviously thought what she'd just said was hilarious.

"She was very sorry she couldn't make it tonight, but she's a grandmother with babysitting duties."

Christ. A grandmother. Micky wasn't sure Sheryl was

doing a good job selling Martha to Amber by saying that.

"Anyway, she asked if I could give you her number."

"I'm not so sure that's a good idea," Amber said.

"Why not?" Sheryl drank from the glass of water Kristin had given her earlier.

"I haven't had a chance to speak to Micky about it," Amber said.

"Micky is sitting here smitten as a kitten with Robin," Sheryl said.

Then Kristin arrived and put her hands on her partner's shoulder. "I think someone's had enough," she said. "Come on, babe. I'll take you upstairs."

"Things are just getting interesting, honey." Sheryl looked up at Kristin. Her eyes narrowed, then her chin dropped and she rose. "I bid you all adieu." She pointed at Amber. "Let me know, okay?"

"So that was the *erudite professor* you told me about," Robin said, her voice dripping with sarcasm.

"She likes a drink. Don't we all?" Micky was starting to see through the perfect exterior of Kristin and Sheryl's relationship. "What did you want to talk to me about, Amber?" she asked, not wanting to gossip about her employer's partner's drinking habits too much.

"I haven't seen you in days. Let's catch up soon," Amber said. "I have an early class tomorrow, so I'd better head home."

"I guess it's just us then," Robin said after Amber had left. "Want to come back to my place for a bit?"

"Oh God, please don't ask me that."

"Just for half an hour. Forty-five minutes tops." When Robin cocked her head like that and smiled that seductive smile, Micky couldn't possibly say no.

★ ★ ★

"I won't see you all weekend?" Robin asked while she peppered Micky's neck with kisses. "Not even on the sly?"

"Don't ask me that while you kiss me like this," Micky

said in between groans.

"You're making me feel like a teenager again, with all this sneaking around." Robin pulled away from her and looked her in the eye. They'd barely made it inside Robin's flat. Micky stood with her back against the front door.

Micky had made a point of writing down Olivia and Christopher's schedule for the weekend, something she had never done before, but neither one of them seemed to have a lot going on in the coming two days, at least not at overlapping times. Either way, it was more a psychological barrier for Micky. When the children were with her, she didn't spend every last second in their company. She had felt compelled to do that post-divorce, but they'd quickly made it clear that they didn't want their mother around all the time. Anyway, this wasn't a matter of proximity. The issue was what Micky was doing when she was out of the house. She wouldn't just need to tell Darren soon, she'd need to inform her children—and her mother.

"I promise it won't be like this for long, but…" Micky always involuntarily smiled when she looked at Robin, especially when Robin's body was half pressed against her like that. "Why not enjoy the excitement that comes with it for now?"

Micky pulled Robin close for a kiss and lost herself in their lip-lock. When, way too soon, the time came for her to leave, her clothes were all ruffled and her acute desire had not been sufficiently quenched—because despite the quickie they'd just had, Micky's hunger for Robin was so bottomless that half an hour alone with her didn't even come close to satisfying it—but she walked home with a spring in her step and a blush on her cheeks nonetheless.

They were together now, and at least for the night, before she had to face the world again in the morning and the prospect of coming out, she could luxuriate in the glowing heat running beneath her flesh that resulted from time spent with Robin.

Micky was in love, and she felt it in every cell of her body.

CHAPTER TWENTY-FOUR

"So," Micky said. "Should I give Sheryl your number to pass on to Martha?" It was Sunday afternoon, and they'd taken Olivia and Chris to Balmoral beach in Mosman where Micky used to spend so much of her time when she was still married. The kids were walking to the beach restaurant with their grandmother to see if they could squeeze them in for dinner tonight.

"I was wondering when you were going to bring that up." Amber stared straight ahead.

"I've tried, Amber, but I just can't shake off the memory of the chemistry crackling in the air between the two of you at that dinner party."

"But she was there for *you*. Sure, at first sight, I did like her, but my mind didn't even go there, I swear to you."

Only Amber would ever feel guilty about something like this. "Well, that really couldn't have gone worse for her, what with Robin showing up like that."

"I know all of that, but… I don't know. It feels weird."

"It may feel weird for half an hour or so, but think of all the time you have left after the feelings of weirdness have subsided. *And*, she's not one of your students."

"Maybe we should organize a group thing again first. Get the initial awkwardness out of the way to see if the spark is still there."

"What are you so afraid of? A beautiful, available woman is interested in you. You should be jumping for joy instead of hesitating like this."

Now Amber did turn her head to look at Micky. "You

know how I've been burned in the past."

"But this is the future." Micky sat up a bit straighter. "You pushed me to put myself out there and be more open to new things, and look at me now. I'm crazy about a gorgeous woman. That's what happened to me because you encouraged me to stop dwelling in the past and to finally face my fears about who I truly am. You did that for me, Amber. Now I'm doing the same for you."

"I know you're right, but for me to be okay with it, I need to let a little bit of time go by. Not long, just a few days, or a week."

Micky sighed. "Nothing happened between Martha and me. We had a forty-five minute conversation alone. That's it."

"That's not true, Micky. You told me about her, and you invited her to your house. I know you're probably thinking this is one of my crazy Amber rules, and it is, but I just need a little bit more time. You're my best friend. I can't just... move in and move on."

"But I'm with Robin now. What does that say about me?"

"We're different people. I'm not judging you, if that's what you want to know. You and Robin, that's an entirely different situation. I do want to go out with Martha. It's been a long time since I met a woman I was so immediately interested in, I just need a little more time."

"I'm already glad you're willing to admit to being attracted to her."

"I didn't say attracted, Micky, I said interested." Amber's facial expression was dead serious.

Micky laughed and shook her head. "Just don't use our friendship as an excuse because what you really are, is afraid to put yourself out there."

"I'm not. But there are other things to consider. Did you hear what Sheryl said? She's a grandmother."

"Well, you're a godmother."

Amber quirked up her eyebrows. "Not the same at all."

"I know, I just fear you're trying to think this to death before anything has even happened."

"That's just how I am. Let's not forget how much time I gave you after your divorce, my dearest friend. You don't think I had to bite my tongue many a time?"

"Er, many a time you didn't."

"Then I at least held off saying what I really wanted to say, while you know that's not my style at all. I was just being a good, considerate, patient friend." Amber let some sand slip through her fingers. "Besides, you've been sleeping with Robin for a few weeks now and you still haven't told me."

"Told you what?" Micky looked at Amber's hands instead of at her face.

"Remember that talk we had a while back about *the spectrum*?"

"I do." Micky dug her fingertips into the sand.

"And how since then you've fallen in love with a woman?"

"Well, yes, which you know all about, so what's left to tell?" Did Amber really need her to say the word?

"I think it would help you a lot to say it out loud. You'll be telling your children soon, Micky. You might as well practice on me."

"You want me to say that I'm a lesbian? That word is really so important to you?" Micky's fingers cramped up in the sand.

"That particular word is of no importance to me whatsoever. It's not about the word. It's about you saying it out loud and, finally, after all these years, admitting it to yourself, and to me."

Micky cleared her throat, looked her best friend in the eye, and said, "I'm in love with a woman. I like women. I guess that makes me a lesbian."

Amber smiled. "Oh, Micky. It's not about what label you stick on yourself or how you identify, it's about you finally just saying it out loud." Amber reached for Micky's hands. "I've seen you struggle with this for such a long time. With all the duties you think you had in regard to everyone. Everyone but yourself. How you pushed aside your own happiness so your family could be happy." She fell silent for a second. "This is an important moment. It really is."

"Maybe it is." It wasn't a hugely cathartic moment, but significant nonetheless. Because what Amber had just said was true, Micky had never admitted it to anyone else, until now. She'd barely admitted it to herself. She looked past Amber's shoulder and saw her mother and the children approach. "But here comes the family." She squared her shoulders and took a deep breath.

Amber let go of her hands but kept looking at her. "When are you going to tell them?"

CHAPTER TWENTY-FIVE

Micky met Darren at the same restaurant he'd told her about Lisa. They didn't sit at the same table, but aside from that, the day could be a reenactment of that very lunchtime conversation—except for one big difference, of course. She would have preferred a more private setting, but privacy wasn't something they had between them anymore.

No matter how deeply she breathed, Micky couldn't get her heartbeat to slow down. It had become a nervous drum inside of her, an insane pitter-patter, reminding her how far out of her comfort zone she was stepping. Because this was Darren. The man who had slept next to her, carefree, safely wrapped up in a cocoon of marital security, for eighteen years.

"Darren will be the easiest one to tell," Amber had assured her. "You don't see him all that often and what he thinks about it doesn't really matter that much in the end." This was true on some level, but as Micky sat across from him, weighing the words in her head—and already having them sound so wrong before they even came out—the intimacy they had shared also made him the hardest person to tell.

"What's going on, Micky?" he asked. "Am I going to need a glass of wine for this?" He held up his glass of sparkling water.

They'd dispensed with the small talk already. They'd discussed the kids' wellbeing. Micky had picked a week when they were with their father to tell him because she would need to see Robin afterward. She would need the time and space to have all these feelings that were wreaking havoc on her common sense re-affirmed.

"I've met someone as well," she blurted out.

Darren set his glass down. "That's great."

Was he really happy for her? Micky was so glad Darren had already met Lisa and had been the first to go through this ordeal of telling the ex-spouse about the new person in his life. But she shouldn't focus on that. She should concentrate on getting the words out. Her heart was full of them, so why was it so hard for them to spill from her mouth?

"Who's the lucky fella?" Darren asked.

Micky could tell his smile wasn't entirely genuine, but he was doing his best. Darren always did his best.

"It's not…" Micky expelled a sigh. "It's not a fella, Darren. Her name is Robin." Being able to say Robin's name emboldened her slightly, but not enough to look her ex-husband in the eye.

When Darren didn't say anything, she had to look away from her hands, otherwise she'd never know what his first reaction had been. He sat there staring, his strong jaw slackened, as though frozen in time just before he was about to say something.

"She works at Goodwin Stark, just like Lisa," Micky said, just to fill the dreadful silence hanging between them.

"You know—" Darren had apparently found the power of speech again. "—I have to say, Micky, this doesn't entirely come as a surprise to me."

"I know you quizzed Amber about my, er, sexuality"— why was that such a hard word to say?—"when things were going south between us. She told me a little while ago."

"Because I didn't know what the hell was going on with you, with us. I know our marriage could have been better at the time, and I was willing to take most of the blame, because you always did all the hard work at home and I was away so much. When you first told me you wanted a divorce,

I truly thought we could fix it, but I had to run through all the options first. That's why I approached Amber." He narrowed his eyes a little. "So I *was* right."

"No, I mean, yes. I've only just recently come to grips with it myself, but I guess, if I'm truly being honest, it was part of the reason why I wanted the divorce." Micky owed Darren as much honesty as she could muster.

"When did you know?" If this information was riling him at all, Darren did an excellent job of hiding it. Perhaps because a year had passed since their divorce, Micky felt more like she was talking to an old friend rather than to her ex-husband.

"I can't pinpoint it exactly. All I can say is that, on some subconscious level, I've known I've been attracted to women for a very long time, but I buried that knowledge so far in the back of my mind, I was successfully able to brush it off as a quirk, as a frivolity, as something unimportant to the life I was leading."

"In a way, I'm glad you're only telling me now. I'm not sure how I would have taken it if you'd given it as the sole reason for our divorce." Darren twirled his fork between his fingers, although, Micky suspected, neither one of them would be eating anymore.

"I was in this strange, almost fugue state, of knowing and not wanting to know at the same time. It was just so hard to admit it to myself because it didn't mesh with who I was. A wife. A mother. Being those two things defined me for eighteen years. They were all I had. I couldn't possibly imagine pulling the rug from underneath the core of my being just because of what I forced myself to think of as a mere frivolity."

"But you did, though. We're divorced. You telling me you no longer wanted to be married to me was quite the rug-pulling. For all of us."

"I know, but what was I supposed to do? Stay and become increasingly unhappy? Because I wasn't happy in that life anymore. I needed to do something, despite the children only being in their teens, and our, to the outside world, perfect life. I knew the identity I had clung to for the past two decades of my life, all my life really, would need to be shattered before I could... I don't know, find my true self. God, I'm beginning to sound like Amber."

"Speaking of Amber. She's your best friend. She's godmother to *both* our children, and she has always been out and proud. Didn't that... give you a nudge?"

"It's not as simple as that. I loved *you*, Darren. Twenty years ago, I fell madly in love with you. That was never something I could push to the side so easily. How could I possibly be attracted to women when I was married to you? When we had two beautiful children. It took a long time for that to make sense in my head, for me to allow myself to even think that this could happen to me, that this could happen to anyone."

"That time I went to see Amber to ask her if you were into women, I didn't really think you were. I was just running around like a chicken with its head cut off, trying to salvage what was left of our marriage." Darren gave a little smile. "Yet, for some reason, this just doesn't come as a huge surprise."

"It hardly surprised Amber either." The coil in Micky's stomach was starting to unfurl a bit, though her heart was still hammering away. "But, er, well, now that I'm seeing someone, I have to tell Liv and Chris."

Darren rubbed his fingers over his brow, then nodded. "Yes, they have a right to know."

Micky could kiss Darren for how extremely understanding he was being about this. For not asking her whether she was sure, or if it wasn't just a phase, and most importantly, for not lamenting his own manhood because his ex-wife was dating another woman. He still was the man she'd fallen for so many years ago. A man with a thoroughly good heart. Though, she guessed, it probably helped that he was in the throes of falling in love himself. It softened him. She remembered the way he had glanced at Lisa at Gigi's.

"You don't think it's too soon?" Micky voiced her own doubts. At times, she thought it was, but sometimes she thought she would just burst—that the news would just explode out of her—if she didn't share it with her children, who lived in her house, who ate the food she prepared for them, who relied on her for so many things, despite the fact that they were teenagers and believed they needed their mother less and less. She couldn't keep it from them for much longer.

"That's really not for me to judge, Micky." Darren started looking at his watch—a habit that used to annoy the hell out of Micky, because it made her feel as though Darren always had somewhere more important to be than in the company of his family.

"Thank you for taking this so well." Micky was starting to find her confidence again. Not counting Amber, because she'd already known, this was her first official coming out, and it was going so much smoother than she had anticipated. Darren wasn't the type to dramatically storm out of a room, on the contrary, but still, this was the sort of news Micky had no idea how anyone would react to. She'd been afraid of reacting herself for so long, she didn't dare imagine other people's reactions.

"How else am I going to take it?" Darren visibly relaxed and fixed his gaze on Micky instead of his watch. "I want you to be happy, Micky. Why else did we go through the hardship of a divorce? If you're happy, Liv and Chris will be happy. Well, at least as happy as sulky teenagers can be." He chuckled at the moodiness of their children. "This may sound very strange coming from your ex-husband, but I think we can look past that now, in light of what you just told me." His eyes lit up. "I know what it feels like to fall in love again. Lisa is just... well, she's amazing; I'd be a fool to not want the same thing to happen to the mother of my children."

"Christ, you really have it bad, don't you?" Micky shot him an easy smile. Maybe this coming-out business would bring her and Darren closer again.

"You've met her. Wouldn't you?"

Micky burst out into a giggle. "The kids seem to like her."

Darren glanced at his watch again. "I'm really sorry, but I have a meeting with my boss in fifteen minutes."

"Okay." *Some things never change.* But she was used to talking to Darren on the clock. "I was thinking about telling them and Mom next weekend. A big lesbian coming-out weekend. They might get so upset they'll want to come stay at yours."

"I'm sure they won't, but I'll be there. Whatever you need." He started to get up.

Micky was so touched by his words of encouragement, that she promptly rose and gave him a hug.

★ ★ ★

"It couldn't have gone any better," Micky said. She'd had the entire afternoon to digest her conversation with Darren and was now sitting at Robin's dining table, eating a dish Robin had prepared for her.

"Nothing fancy," she'd said, "I just want to make you a home-cooked meal on a momentous day like this."

Micky's appetite had flared after as good as skipping lunch. Why had she wanted to come out to Darren over lunch, anyway? She wouldn't make that mistake twice. By the time she was done coming out, she'd be an expert at it. She recognized ricotta and chili peppers in Robin's pasta dish. It was delicious.

She was also still riding the wave of elation that had descended upon her on the way home from lunch. She had been so happy with how the conversation had gone, that she was easily able to bury her skepticism—why wasn't he more upset? More worried about the children? More questioning?

—underneath the sheer joy of feeling the most herself she had in a good long while. After coming home, she'd been so flooded with burst after burst of sky-rocketing self-esteem, that she'd found herself unable to stay indoors and gone for a long, meandering walk around the neighborhood, picking up fresh flowers, even drinking a green juice along the way without having Amber to spur her on. Until Robin, who had promised to knock off work early for the occasion, got home and she watched her lover make dinner.

Lover. Micky had started reading a lesbian fiction novel the other day, and the two women who were falling in love referred to each other that way.

Robin stared at her, a big smile on her face. "That's really great, honey."

Honey. The term of endearment touched Micky disproportionally. Perhaps because her new lesbian lover had just cooked her dinner. After the supreme boost of self-confidence that coming out to Darren had delivered, Micky's emotions were all over the place. She was happier than she'd been in a long time, but that didn't stop her from realizing that her children's happiness was also at stake. She couldn't be completely happy until she'd told them *and* they had reacted in a good way.

"It really is, but I can't relax until Chris and Liv know. So many more steps to take on this road to…" Micky didn't know what to say. She didn't want to sound too overbearing, because Robin might have come back for her that night and set this whole process in motion, but it was mid-April now, the leaves on the trees outside were already starting to turn, which left them with only seven and a half months together. What seemed like an eternity before, because of so many mitigating factors and unspoken feelings and insecurities, now seemed like a cruelly short stretch of time.

"That might be so, Micky, but you're taking the steps, and you're taking them swiftly and confidently, and I'm so proud of you."

"Goodwin Stark's Diversity Manager's lover can hardly be a closet case now, can she?"

Robin pulled her lips into a smile. "Lover? Really?"

"What would you call me?" Micky put down her fork.

"Anything but that. Girlfriend, I guess."

"I'm forty-four years old. Can I really be someone's girlfriend?"

"My woman-friend then," Robin said. "Or my vixen. Or better, my insatiable vixen." Robin wiggled her eyebrows up and down.

"Oh, stop it. I'm trying to have a serious conversation," Micky jokingly berated Robin. "*Lover*."

"Well, then, lover, you'd better live up to your name later." Robin winked at her.

Micky just stared at her blankly.

"Did I freak you out with the prospect of having the entire weekend together to have the most earth-shattering sex?" Robin asked.

"No." A frisson of suspended lust crept up Micky's spine. "It's just that on this day of speaking truths and all that—and I know what I'm about to say is way too premature and silly, but today of all days, it's only apt that I refuse to hold back my true feelings." Dramatically, Micky brought a hand to her chest. "We have this weekend because the kids are at Darren's. There are seven and a half months left in the year, so roughly thirty weekends which, divided by two, gives us fifteen more weekend like this together."

"Will you be counting the orgasms next?" Robin tensed, her neck straightening and that little groove between her eyebrows deepening.

"I'm sorry, but I would be lying if I sat here and claimed I don't have a problem with this, with us and the time we have left together, being finite. And I know I'm moving too fast, I'm truly well aware of it, but I feel I have so much life to catch up on that it seems to be the only way to go for me. I'll be introducing you to my children soon, and whatever will I say to them? Meet Robin, my short-term lover?" As soon as she was done pouring out her heart, a wave of anguish traveled through Micky. She knew this was the opposite of what Robin wanted. Robin had told her this was exactly the sort of drama she wanted to avoid. But damn it, Robin had been the one to come knocking on *her* door, steeped in the knowledge that Micky would never turn her away. Grand gestures followed by obliterating climaxes were all well and good, but what would Micky end up with ultimately? She didn't need the broken heart that saying good-bye to Robin would cause.

"Hey." Robin's hand traveled the width of the table, then reached for Micky's. "Things have changed for me too. I know I said all those things to you, and they were true for me at the time, but I do also distinctly remember saying that I had never met anyone for whom I wanted to stay and alter the course of my life. And, oh yes, it's still early days and way too soon to start talking about this in other than vague terms, but I'm unattached, Micky. The biggest reason for me wanting to move back home at the end of the year is to plant roots, to not have to up-end my life every time my job takes me elsewhere, but nothing is set in stone, and who knows, maybe by then I will have planted some roots here?"

"Wow." Micky couldn't remember a lot of times in her life when she'd been rendered speechless—only when, bone-tired after labor, her children had been carefully deposited in the cradle of her arms—but this was definitely one of them.

"Life can be funny that way," Robin said and squeezed Micky's hand a little tighter.

Whatever happened to no strings attached?

CHAPTER TWENTY-SIX

The next Saturday afternoon, Micky invited her mother and Amber over for tea. No big meals would be served, but they would need something to do with themselves. Pastries would do the trick. Amber would be there for moral support. Both the kids and her mother held Amber in such high regard—and she was a lesbian.

"This is very unusual, dear," her mother said when she arrived. "Do you and Amber have a special announcement to make?" Then she caught sight of her grandchildren, both hanging on the sofa with their headphones on. "Best get those off before Amber arrives."

Micky's mother occupied herself with asking how the kids were doing in school while Micky put on the kettle. This was it. Between then and an hour, it would all be out in the open. The knot in her stomach reminded her of how she felt when she and Darren had told the kids about the divorce, though, objectively, this was such happier news she was about to deliver.

The bell rang, and before Micky had a chance to say anything, Olivia shot up and yelled she would get it. Her children effectively already admired a lesbian woman. What could they possibly have against their mother being one?

If only it were that easy.

As Amber came in and said her hellos, exchanging a meaningful glance with her, Micky wondered—again—if she'd made the right decision of telling her mother and her children at the same time. After telling Darren, and the nice things Robin had said to her throughout the week that followed, it had been a quick and easy decision to make. Kill two birds with one stone *while* still riding that high of her first unexpectedly successful and—admittedly—heartwarming coming out.

Micky felt as though, if she didn't tell the most important people in her life as soon as possible, her luck would run out. Having them all together in a room, with Amber there to reply to any questions Micky wasn't knowledgeable enough or too self-conscious to answer, would make it easier for them to process together. But now, as everyone found their preferred spot on the sofa, she doubted her decision. Perhaps she should have confided in her mother separately. Then, she stopped herself. Micky should have and could have done a lot of things differently in her life. This was where it had gotten her, and really, the most important was that they all knew. That she didn't have to walk around feeling guilty all the time for keeping this vital piece of information to herself.

She poured the grown-ups some tea. Chris sipped from a Diet Coke, much to his sister's dismay, who got that particular sentiment about her brother drinking diet soda from Amber.

"This all seems very official. I'm starting to worry," her mother said.

"There's no need to worry. Nobody is sick or dying." Micky fidgeted with a packet of sugar. "I, er, just need to tell you something."

They all stared at her with expectation in their eyes. For comfort, Micky looked at Amber, who nodded at her almost imperceptibly.

She addressed her children. "You know how your dad introduced you to Lisa a few weeks ago? Well, I've met someone too."

Just the night before, Micky had sort of rehearsed this moment with Amber, who had advised her to not practice too much but simply speak from the heart and, perhaps, break the news about Robin slowly. All night and all morning, Micky had practiced a, what she thought, well-balanced but to-the-point speech in her head, only to forget all about it when she needed the words to roll off her tongue now.

Nobody spoke. They were all still watching her as though she was playing a part in the most exciting thriller they'd seen in years.

Micky found Amber's gaze, but no, she had to look her children in the eye when she told them. Because what did it say about her if she couldn't even do that? That she was ashamed of who she really was?

"Her name is Robin. I met her at The Pink Bean. She works at a bank, just like your dad."

Christopher's eyes grew wide while Olivia screwed hers shut for an instant.

"But…" Chris started but didn't continue.

"Goodness me," her mother said.

"I know this is a lot to take in and that for you"—Micky made a swooping gesture with her hand—"it must come totally out of the blue, but, er, I've been having these feelings for a while and it's no longer right to keep that from you."

"You're dating a woman?" Chris was the first of her children to find his voice again. "For how long?"

"Is that why you and dad got a divorce?" Olivia asked.

"It's not you, is it?" Gina asked Amber, obviously not having properly absorbed the mention of Robin's name.

Amber just shook her head solemnly.

"You must have many questions, and I will do my best to answer them all, but I need you to know that this is not something I've been hiding from all of you for a long time. It's new to me as well. Falling in love with another woman has been—" Micky had to stop herself there. Because this wasn't about Robin and how hard Micky had fallen for her, this was about her and her family. "Robin and I have been seeing each other for a couple of weeks, so not very long. You can meet her if you want, but you don't have to. And, Liv, honey, your question is very difficult because I can't really give a straight answer to that. Your dad and I got divorced because our marriage wasn't working anymore, and I'd be lying if I said that all of this had nothing to do with it whatsoever, but marriages end for a whole bunch of reasons and this was just one of many."

"I would certainly like to meet this... Robin," Gina said, then turned to Amber again. "Did you have anything to do with this?"

"Amber has nothing to do with it. It's not because she's a lesbian that I suddenly became one." If her children hadn't been present, Micky might have tried explaining the spectrum to her mother, but she deemed it inappropriate— not so much for children's ears, but because it involved their mother.

Liv and Chris sat there, leaning back in the sofa, with a stupefied look on their faces. Poor things. They'd never seen it coming.

"Is she your first, then?" Gina asked, making Micky truly wish she'd told her mother on a separate occasion. She'd overlooked the fact that she would have questions of a different nature, and she'd also believed, wrongly it appeared now, that her children would find comfort in their grandmother's presence, in not having to face the news alone.

"Yes, Mom, she is." Micky couldn't keep a hint of annoyance from creeping into her tone.

"I don't understand," Olivia said. "You were married to dad for so long. You're not like auntie Amber, who's been gay forever. How can it just change like that?"

"How, I don't know, honey, but well, people can change over time and fall in love with totally different people in the course of their lives, even people of a different sex."

"I hope you're not rushing into anything just because

Darren has a girlfriend now," Gina said. Of all three of them, she seemed to be taking it the hardest. Or perhaps she was just better at translating her shock—and other emotions—into words.

"It has nothing to do with Darren." *And I met Robin* before *he even told me about Lisa*, Micky added, in a very petulant voice, in her head.

"I would like to meet her as well." Christopher's voice was confident. "So what if it's with another woman? I just want you to be happy, Mom."

Micky felt a tear pearl in the corner of her eye at the words from her beautiful boy. His reaction she had been afraid of the least, perhaps because he was the eldest of her children and he understood the most. And he'd always been a bit of a mommy's boy. His comment earned him an eye roll from his sister, though.

"Thank you, Chris. That means a lot." Micky wanted to get up and give him a long hug.

"Whereas I will need some time to process this information about my only child," Gina said. She'd barely touched her tea. Now, she rose and started looking around for her purse.

"Liv, Chris, why don't I take you guys out for some fro-yo so your mom and granny can talk," Amber said. She rose and made for the door and, in between, caught Micky's gaze and mouthed *I've got this.*

★ ★ ★

"I'm your mother, Michaela," Gina said, "and I didn't have the faintest idea." After Amber had ushered the kids out of the house, her mother had sat back down. "You used to always tell me what was going on with you."

"I didn't tell you sooner because I was still figuring it out myself." Perhaps this was the hardest part for Micky. She hadn't just one day woken up and realized she only wanted to be with women for the rest of her life. It had been a slow, gradual process of small lightbulbs going off, often with years in between them, and finally illuminating a path for Micky through the darkness in which the desires of her subconscious mind had been cast.

"But you and Darren were married for eighteen years. I think that's what baffles me the most. You were always happy, Micky. Up until a few years ago, when you lost some of your luster. I never gave you a hard time about the divorce because it's not my place and I'd like to think you have a decent head on your shoulders and you knew what you were doing, but this... this I can't understand."

"The information is still so new. You're still absorbing the shock. At least I've had time to get used to it—it took me years, in fact, to get to this point. I don't expect you to throw your arms around me and tell me you understand. I'm as much a realist as you."

Gina nodded. "Just for the record, I love Amber, and I have no moral or other objections to her lifestyle. You know that. I'm not some homophobic bigot, I just... as your mother, I can't help but question this. Are you sure, Micky? Isn't this just some midlife thing? How old is this woman, anyway?"

"Not that much younger than I am." How could Micky possibly explain that being with Robin felt so right, so satisfying, so like coming home after a lifetime of traveling nowhere, that she felt it in every cell of her body? "And no, I can assure you it's not a midlife crisis, even though I have the age for it."

"What did Darren say?" Gina kept fidgeting, her glance skittering around the room. This was a hard conversation for her to have as well, Micky imagined. She could only hope the hard line of questioning would soon make way for softer words of understanding.

"He was happy for me." Micky tried to hold her mother's gaze but failed.

"I'm not trying to give you a hard time here. I'm just trying to make sense of this. You're my daughter and I love you more than words could ever say, and of course I want you to be happy, I just…" Gina fell silent. At seventy-three, she was still a striking woman, but suddenly, startlingly, she looked her age. As though Micky's news had accelerated some processes inside of her that had been magically slowed before.

"It's okay, Mom. You need time to digest."

"I would like to meet her. It must be serious if you're telling the kids about her."

Define serious, Micky wanted to say. Of course, she was very serious about Robin, but that didn't change the fact that it was still early days for them. "She's pretty amazing," Micky said, failing to keep her voice from sounding schmaltzy.

"Set it up then. I'll be there with bells on *and* on my best behavior. I'm a Ferro, after all, you know I can turn it on for anyone."

Micky knew it was meant as a joke—an inside joke they'd had between them forever—but still, it came out wrong. She was, however, in no position to demand an apology from her mother. Micky was also pretty certain that Robin would have no problem charming Gina Ferro.

"I watch *Wentworth* too, you know," Gina said. "They're all lesbians in that prison."

Micky broke out in a chuckle. "Don't worry, Mom. They won't throw me in prison for falling in love with a woman."

✱ ✱ ✱

"I think they just can't imagine it," Micky said. It was the day after she'd told her children and her mother, and she lay with her head in Robin's lap, looking up at her. "Or they have all sorts of images running through their head of things that they should never imagine their mother doing."

"You've done your part." Robin was stroking her hair. "You've told them. They know you're there for them if they have questions. That is really all you can do. It's up to them now."

"I keep thinking about how easy they were about Darren and Lisa. It's so unfair. Why should it even still matter in this day and age? Aren't we all supposed to be so much more evolved now?"

"Says the woman who took ages to admit to herself she had feelings for other women."

"All I was waiting for was for the right woman to turn up in my life."

"And there I was, ordering a wet cappuccino in The Pink Bean. Imagine if you hadn't taken that job. We might have never met."

"I'd be going out with Martha."

"Much to Amber's dismay," Robin said.

"Christ, imagine the drama. Me dating Martha and Amber having the hots for her. She's already so reluctant to do anything about it now, because she's Amber and these things always have to be a huge deal, and thoroughly talked through and whatnot."

"Maybe Martha would have dumped you for Amber." Robin smirked down at her.

"Are you saying I can't keep a woman? You? Who brushed me off only to come rushing back to me because I'm so irresistible." Micky found Robin's hands and braided her fingers through hers.

"You are, you know. Irresistible. Maybe it's because you're Italian. I've always had a thing for the darker-haired, more exotic chicks."

"Oh yeah?" Micky couldn't stop gazing into Robin's bright blue eyes. "How many chicks are we talking about here, now that we're on the subject?"

Robin laughed heartily, making Micky's head shudder in her lap. "More than you've had, that's for sure."

"Seriously." Micky brought their joined hands to her belly and kept them there.

"You really want to know how many women I've been with? Because I would have to sit down and count. I've been at this lesbian thing for a while."

"Next you'll tell me you'll need a calculator."

"I just might." Robin keeled forward and kissed Micky on the forehead. "But hey, those spectacular orgasms you've been having are only the result of my vast experience."

"Oh, please, Robin. Your orgasms don't seem any less spectacular than mine, and I'm a beginner. Your argument doesn't hold up. You've been slutting it up for years, you might as well admit it."

"And you best be careful what you say." Robin's interlaced fingers suddenly grabbed down hard, squashing Micky's hand in a painful but not unpleasant grip. "Or I'll have to punish you."

Micky was still looking up at Robin, whose features had gone a bit more serious, though her eyes still sparkled. "I'd like to see you try."

Robin scrunched her lips together. "You asked for it." She let go of Micky's hand, pulled up Micky's top, and started tickling her mercilessly, her fingers running over Micky's skin, making it impossible for her to remain still.

Somehow, Robin ended up on top of her. Micky's blouse had ridden all the way up and her abs hurt from giggling uncontrollably.

Fuck, I'm happy, she thought. *I'm so incredibly happy.* She didn't say anything, just pulled Robin close to her and kissed her for a long time, until darkness started falling outside— autumn really was creeping closer—and she had to hurry home before the kids got back from the movie they were seeing with Amber.

"Shall I go with you?" Robin asked, after Micky had meticulously smoothed down her clothes and finger-combed her hair back into shape.

Micky didn't know if Robin was joking. "Not just yet," she said. "Maybe in two weeks, after they've had a week at their dad's and more time to come to terms with it."

Robin got up from the sofa and walked over to Micky.

"If they're anything like their mother, they'll be head-over-heels with me in no time." She kissed Micky on the cheek so sweetly, that Micky didn't want to leave anymore.

CHAPTER TWENTY-SEVEN

Micky had made it clear to Christopher and Olivia that she was there for them if they had any questions, but after the weekend, they had quickly reverted to their habit of spending most of their home time in their bedrooms. When Olivia wasn't around, Chris continued to assure her that he had no issues with what Micky had told him, while Olivia appeared to still be stuck in a let's-pretend-that-conversation-never-happened phase.

Micky thought it best not to force either one to talk about it and give them—and especially Liv—the time they needed to adjust to this new, other side of their mother. But it was only the next Wednesday morning when she went into their rooms before heading to work the way she always did, to make sure they were awake and had all their stuff packed before going to their dad's for the next week, that she realized how much tension had been hanging in the air in the house.

Since the divorce, Micky had always dreaded Wednesdays because they were change-over day, but this particular Wednesday, for the very first time, she felt an odd kind of relief at having the house to herself for a week. Because, it hit her, she *had* been walking on eggshells, and she had been feeling guilty for changing her children's view about their mother once again. Micky had already upended their lives once and ruptured the stable home environment they'd always enjoyed. Now, once more, she was asking them to accept more change, while all they wanted, she guessed, after finding their feet again in a new neighborhood and at a new school, was for everything to stay the same, at least for a little while.

But Micky didn't believe in the sort of motherhood that sacrificed everything for the children. She'd divorced Darren to "find her truth," as Amber would call it, to "walk her own path" and she would never have done that if she didn't truly believe that, in the end, her children could only benefit from seeing their mother at her happiest. Now especially, after having told them about Robin, she had to hold on to that. Because no matter how much the news had upped the level of tension in the house and brought up another subject her son and daughter disagreed on, for Micky, a sense of relief was starting to set in.

She'd only gone and had the most difficult conversation of her life. Sure, she could probably have done it better, been more eloquent, injected more patience into her tone when she'd talked to her own mother, but nobody was perfect. They weren't actors in a TV movie, where, after a big reveal like that, the heroine worded her feelings in a perfectly understandable way that moved her family members to the point that the only outcome was complete, instant acceptance and teary hugs.

"Bye, honey," she said to Chris, who still had the covers pulled over his head. She walked into his room, sat down on the edge of his bed briefly and planted a kiss where she thought his face would be. "I love you."

He grumbled something she didn't understand. Micky had never been that much of a morning person herself, but the way teenagers could overdramatize having to get up early in the morning was quite impressive.

She hesitated in front of Liv's room, knocked twice, and when no answer came she opened the door. Olivia was up already, staring at her phone screen.

"Hey, you," Micky said, ignoring the fact that Olivia hadn't replied to her knock on the door. Being a mother to teenagers equaled being able to forgive their impoliteness as instantly as it occurred. "Are you okay?" Micky leaned against the doorframe.

"I didn't sleep very well," Olivia mumbled.

"How come?"

Olivia just shrugged, but Micky knew to give her some time to articulate her thoughts.

"Everything's changing. Dad's got Lisa and you…" She huffed out some air. "You're a *lesbian* now." She barely pronounced the l-word.

Micky headed into her daughter's room and parked her behind on the edge of the bed. "I know it's a lot, honey." She brushed a strand of Olivia's bedhead hair away from her face. "So much change all at once, and it may feel unfair, but it will all work out in the end, I promise you that."

"No it won't, because now you and dad will never get back together," Liv blurted out.

"Is that really what you want? For your dad and me to get back together?" Olivia had never expressed that wish before.

"I don't know, Mom. All I know is that how things are now isn't exactly what I've been dreaming of."

Micky scooted a little closer and put a hand on Olivia's shoulder. "I know, honey." Micky was about to apologize, but how could she possibly say sorry for falling in love with a woman and the subsequent happiness that had taken hold of her? She just had to keep believing that, in time, Olivia would understand this was all for the best. Though, looking at her, as she sat so frumpily in bed, looking a couple of years younger than her fourteen years, Micky felt a pang of guilt rush through her again for not putting her children's happiness before hers. "It's going to be okay." Micky didn't know what else to do but utter a few generic phrases. Olivia was still so young and vulnerable and susceptible. She still needed her mother to tell her this. "I promise you." She pulled Liv in an awkward hug and said, "I love you so, so much."

✶ ✶ ✶

At The Pink Bean, Josephine was missing in action due to some long-announced activity at the university she had to attend. Micky had assured Kristin she could handle the morning rush by herself by now, but she sure was glad that Kristin was there to help.

Micky had discussed her weekend of coming out with her boss quite a few times over the course of that week already, but the conversation with Olivia was still fresh on her mind and Kristin had become some wise lesbian guru to her who held the answers to many questions.

"Despite being well into the twenty-first century and the great leaps in acceptance that have occurred over the last decade alone, we still live in a heteronormative society," Kristin said during a break. "It's what 99 percent of children still grow up seeing all around them and accepting as the one true way."

Micky had to chuckle at the irony. "That's exactly how my children grew up, despite having a lesbian woman as a godmother."

"There's only so much influence a single person can exercise." Kristin looked so well put-together again, as though her clothes were freshly laundered this morning, and her subtle makeup had been applied by a professional. "But there's some excellent literature on the subject and you know that Sheryl teaches gender studies. If you want to give them a broader perspective, I'm sure she wouldn't mind talking to them. You know how she loves to talk."

With a nice bottle of wine by her side. Micky berated herself for that instantly. "That might be a good idea. And either way, it won't hurt them to get to know a few more lesbians."

"Sheryl and I have a bunch of nieces and nephews, and I can assure you that they are the best-educated young adults on gender- and queer-related topics." Kristin smiled. "She even managed to convince my very conservative Korean parents to embrace the fact that their daughter was never going to marry a respectable man. And this was years ago. But I guess when someone with Sheryl's natural gravitas and intense stare looks at you and tells you it's okay to be gay, you just can't argue against that." Kristin chuckled. "And once she's on her soapbox, it's really hard to get her off. Unless you're waving around a bottle of 1999 Barossa Shiraz."

Micky didn't know what to say to that last remark, so she focused on what Kristin had said before. "I would really appreciate Sheryl taking the time to do that. Between her and Amber, my kids don't stand a chance of not accepting the fact that their mother has a lesbian lover." Micky was so grateful to be able to discuss all of this so openly at her workplace and with her boss, who was quickly turning into a good friend.

"In the end, the most important thing they'll need is some time to adjust to the idea. They'll come around once they see how happy Robin makes you, Micky."

"Hm," Micky hummed. She couldn't wait to see Robin that night and to be able to spend every night with her until her children returned the following Wednesday.

CHAPTER TWENTY-EIGHT

"There's nothing more I want from this weekend than to lie naked with you in bed," Micky said. She might have only worked part-time at The Pink Bean, but this week, after all the emotional turmoil of the previous weekend and having taken calls from her mother every other day to ask whether she was still a lesbian, Micky was exhausted. And despite the brief sense of relief that came with the kids staying at their dad's, she had missed them much more than during other weeks.

"That can easily be arranged." Robin smiled at her. She'd come straight over to Micky's house after attending good-bye drinks for a colleague. Her eyes were a little watery, and from the way she was slightly slurring her words, Micky concluded she was quite tipsy. Micky had fed her a healthy Moroccan vegetable stew that Amber had once showed her how to make. It was now one of Micky's easy go-to dishes when she was tired but wanted to ingest some nutrients instead of getting fast food, which had been Amber's argument exactly when she'd given Micky the recipe. Her dear old friend Amber. Micky had no idea what her life would be like if it weren't for Amber. Would she ever have found the courage to even admit her true desires to herself?

"You don't look like you'll be able to stay awake very long tonight, though, babe," Micky teased. "You've been hard at work managing diversity all week."

Robin nodded. "This guy who is leaving, at first they weren't going to replace him, but now there's talk of perhaps combining his position with mine, which could possibly lead to a more permanent job for me here."

Micky's eyes grew wide. "Really?"

"It's a possibility. Goodwin Stark is not a small corporation, and it's definitely not a done deal yet. And you know how HR people love to blab on about career possibilities and positive changes and so on and so forth, but there's talk."

"You can tell whoever has the final say about this that Michaela Ferro, of the Mosman Ferros, is petitioning for you to stay for a good long while."

Robin chuckled. "I'm petitioning for Michaela Ferro to take her ass upstairs and take off all her clothes."

Micky glanced at Robin. She looked a little disheveled and a lot tired, but to her, she was still the most beautiful woman she had ever seen. "Sure, but I'm setting a timer to see how long my naked ass will be able to keep you awake."

"You're forgetting that I'm still a long way away from being forty. I have stamina." Robin broadened her chest and beat her fists against them like a gorilla.

"Why don't *you* get your ass upstairs then and show *me*," Micky challenged.

"I shall." Robin hopped off her chair and bounded up the stairs.

By the time Micky had put the half-empty bottle of wine in the fridge, rinsed a few dishes, and made it to her bedroom, Robin was cozily tucked in, only her head peeking out from under the sheets; her eyes looked heavy-lidded, as though she was seconds away from drifting into the most long-awaited of sleeps.

Micky slipped out of her clothes and under the covers with Robin, still astounded by the instant comforting effect a warm body in her bed had on her, and gazed at her *lover*. "Sleep tight, honeybun." She kissed her on the nose and turned off the lights. They had all weekend to do what Micky had, again, been thinking of all day.

✳ ✳ ✳

Micky was awakened by the sound of water cascading down. Robin was already up and about. Before taking the job at The Pink Bean, Micky would have been up well before eight on a Saturday morning, but nowadays she often slept until after nine. She stretched her arms over her head, and as she did, an idea popped into her mind. She jumped out of bed and tiptoed to the bathroom. The glass shower cabin was entirely fogged up, and from what she could make out, Robin had her back to the door. One of the features of the house that had made Micky fall in love with it on the spot, had been the huge shower. Not that back then she had any idea of what might occur in it, but she was about to put it to good use. She opened the door and slipped in behind Robin.

"Oh my God," Robin shrieked. "You nearly gave me a heart attack."

"Who? You? Who is still such a long way away from forty?" She wrapped her arms around Robin's slick-skinned waist. "Anyway, I'm about to give you something much better than a heart attack."

Robin turned around in her embrace, and their lips locked. Micky ran her fingers over Robin's soaped-up back, enjoying the smooth feel of it on her fingertips. She really did want to do nothing else than this all weekend long.

"Obviously I need to wash you first," Robin said when their lips broke apart. "Come on. Hands above your head. Legs wide. I need to get into every nook and cranny."

Micky shook her head. "You are so bossy, do you know that?"

Robin tipped her head to the side. "I might have heard that before."

"Here's the deal," Micky said. "You can wash me all you want, but after that, I'm the boss. My house, my rules." Something took root in her stomach. Something indefinable but incredibly arousing.

"We'll see." Robin smiled, then turned to squirt some soap into the palm of her hands. She rubbed her hands together, then applied the soap to Micky's skin, starting with her belly and working her way up to her breasts without wasting any time.

Robin's hands fluttered over her shoulders and her back next, but they kept coming back to Micky's breasts, as though drawn to them by an invisible, irresistible force.

"I think my breasts are clean now," Micky whispered, apparently no longer able to use her full voice.

Robin's eyes found hers, while her fingers locked onto Micky's nipples. She didn't say anything and instead, just intensified her grip and squeezed tight.

"Ow," Micky yelped.

Robin lifted her eyebrows. "That's what you get for giving me lip." Her hands slickly meandered away from Micky's breasts and found her buttocks, then she pulled Micky closer, their skin meeting in a wet, soapy embrace. *So many new thrills.* The sensation was exquisite. The next thing she knew, Robin pushed her backward against the glass shower wall and kneeled in front of her. She soaped up Micky's legs and thighs, her slender fingers skimming her skin, leaving Micky wet inside and out.

"That should do it." Robin took a step back and admired her handiwork, then reached for the showerhead and let the water rain down Micky's shoulders. Her free hand followed the direction of the water, dedicating a lot of time to her breasts again, and all the while, Micky's heartbeat kept accelerating, because this was quite possibly the most arousing experience of her life.

Robin then lowered the showerhead to rinse Micky's legs, only to turn its nozzle upside down at the apex of Micky's thighs and unleash its strong jet of water on her clit. Micky's muscles stiffened. She had let the showerhead linger in places before, where its relentless stream felt good, and briefly luxuriated in the short, mild sort of pleasure it provided—more a fleeting tingle passing through her than anything else—but she'd never deliberately aimed it there with the sole purpose of coming. Somehow, that had always seemed too far a possibility, too much like something someone like Micky didn't do.

But here she stood, and oh, the jets of water seemed to hit the spot so much more precisely than when she handled the showerhead herself. Robin's presence had a lot to do with that. That intense gleam she'd had in her eyes when she was running her hands all over Micky, never wavering, always so clear in its intent. When Micky looked in Robin's eyes there was never any doubt about how much Robin wanted her. She made Micky feel like the most desirable woman on the face of the earth. And all of that while Micky had the supreme privilege of ogling Robin's firm, strong body. She could stare at that subtle outline of abs all day long, let her fingers roam over that shoulder line for hours on end.

Oh Christ, Micky felt her legs go a little weak at the knees. The water massaged her clit in the most direct, exquisite way, and soon Micky started feeling the familiar heat claw its way up from deep within her core. Could some water pointed in the right direction really do that to her? Or was this all Robin once again?

The heat was about to hit the surface of her skin when Robin plunged a finger deep inside of Micky. The jet kept blasting, and Robin's finger curled, and pressed, and delved, and Micky was about to lose her mind. There was something about the combination of the water hitting her with full force and the way Robin was fucking her that made for the strangest, most unstoppable sensation inside of her. Micky was familiar with the glorious climaxes Robin had given her thus far, but this was different. The approaching orgasm felt more inevitable, more profound, and coming from a place so deep inside her, it made Micky's legs tremble.

Then it overtook her, and Micky's mind went pitch-black while her muscles spasmed and the red hot tingle spread through her flesh and quaked its way through her every fiber and... what the hell? As she came to, Micky could swear she felt a hot trickle of water run down her inner thighs that didn't spout from the showerhead. In fact, Robin had pointed the shower away from her body, and yet Micky felt something leaking from inside of her. She cast her eyes down in amazement, but there was nothing to see, really, because she was standing in the shower and everything around her was wet anyway.

Robin refitted the showerhead in its hook and wrapped her arms around Micky. "Are you okay?" she asked, her tone a little high-pitched.

"Yeah." Micky was panting, still coming down from that strange but intensely pleasing climax. "I just, I don't know, felt something I've never felt before."

"What?" Robin insisted.

"Like trickle after trickle of fluid coming out of me while I came."

Robin drew her lips into a small smile. She kissed Micky on the cheek. "You squirted, babe. That's pretty amazing and a whole lot of sexy."

"It felt great but also, well, a little confusing," Micky admitted.

Robin nodded. "The showerhead did that to you, huh? Can't wait to see how you react to my vibrator." Robin kissed her full on the lips, then trailed her mouth to Micky's ear. "Your lesbian sexual awakening is such a massive turn on for me," she said.

★ ★ ★

After toweling each other dry, Micky still a little dazed because of what happened in the shower, they lay in bed, and she remembered what she'd said to Robin earlier. She was going to be the boss. What had she even meant by that? It had just been an instinctive reaction to how Robin always was. So confident, so self-assured in her every move and word—not a small part of Micky's attraction to her. And now what? Was she supposed to tie Robin's wrists to the bedposts with a scarf hastily dug up from a drawer? She pushed all thoughts of Robin's bound wrists, the notion of it causing a slight throb between her legs nonetheless, to the back of her mind, toppled onto her side, and ran a finger over Robin's taut stomach.

"Would you really stay in Sydney for me?" she asked. Because long after Robin had fallen asleep, a gentle alcohol-induced purr escaping from her lips as she breathed, Micky had considered Robin's words.

"Depends," Robin replied, "on what that finger of yours does next." A smirk split her lips.

Micky didn't have that much experience with falling in love, but there was no doubt they were in the depths of that *phase* she read about in every women's magazine. The early stages of a brand new relationship, where love and lust blended into an ever-present compulsion to touch each other, to please each other, to be with each other every second of the day.

"Ah, so it's a sex thing," Micky said, pretending to be offended.

"As I said before, you're my insatiable vixen, my sexy cougar. All jokes aside, Micky, I love your voracious hunger for me. I love that how much you want me is so visible on your face. Truth be told, I love that I'm your first woman, that I'm the one who makes you feel this way." She followed up with a giggle. "And I especially love that you squirted for me."

Micky shook her head. She didn't say anything. She figured that anything she'd say next would just elicit more innuendo and back talk from Robin. And who was she kidding, anyway? She wanted her finger to caress every inch of Robin's skin, wanted to make it do what Robin's finger had done to her earlier. She traced it up to Robin's breasts, up to her nipples, and lightly skated the tip of her index finger over them. Oh, Micky knew exactly what to do to shut Robin up—and she would be plenty bossy in her own way, and torture Robin in the most delicious way in the process.

Micky found Robin's gaze as her finger applied the lightest of pressure. The only flaw in the plan that she'd just hatched to drive Robin insane with lust ever so slowly was that merely touching Robin always ignited a whole slew of lustful processes inside of herself. Despite the climax she'd just had in the shower, Micky's clit began to pulse in tune with her heartbeat again, rapid and zestful. Come to think of it, she really was Robin's insatiable vixen, although, truly, that was just one part of it. Undeniable attraction had brought them together, even after deciding they weren't suited for each other, but Micky was much more than this body filled with desire she lived in.

She was an out lesbian now.

Micky traced her finger to Robin's other breast, catching a drop of water she'd missed when she'd dried her off. She circled Robin's nipple until it rose up for her as though wanting to meet her finger. Micky leaned over and pecked it lightly, then brushed her tongue against it, before letting it slip between her lips gingerly. Robin was already starting to moan and grind. Micky kissed her way to Robin's other nipple and lavished it with the gentle attention of her tongue and lips. Her finger wandered down, encircling Robin's belly button and drawing an invisible line above her pubic hair.

"Micky, come on," Robin gasped. She was always so impatient. Micky was almost certain she'd be grabbing her hand in the next few seconds and would start pushing it down. But Micky wanted to take advantage of the fact that they had all day, all weekend, to do this. She wanted for the image of Robin's immaculate skin and shapely form to be etched on the back of her eyelids by the time she left for work on Monday. Because now that Micky was finally able to admit to herself that this was what she'd wanted for the longest time, she wanted everything all the time, and if she couldn't be with Robin physically, she would at least be thinking about her, and the way she lay there right now, her legs spreading already.

Micky peppered kisses on Robin's belly, her lips barely touching Robin's skin, not going any lower than the top of the triangle of her pubic hair.

"Oh, Micky, I want you," Robin moaned.

As her confidence as a lover had grown, Micky found herself better able to withstand Robin's pleas to fuck her, and today especially, Micky took great pleasure in Robin's begging tone. It illustrated how much Robin wanted her, and really, Micky could never get enough of that.

"Oh, screw it," Robin said and pushed herself up. She drew her legs up and toppled onto her knees. Before Micky had the chance to find her bearings—and berate Robin for her extreme lack of patience—Robin was pulling Micky toward her, and automatically, Micky mirrored her position. She sat across from Robin on her knees, her legs spread, their breasts touching.

"I need you now," Robin said.

Micky shook her head. "You're incorrigible."

"Let's see what you have to say about that after I do this." Robin brought her hand in between Micky's legs and, while she looked her in the eye, slipped two fingers inside.

Micky's breath hitched in her throat. *Always so bossy*, she thought, until she stopped thinking.

"Fuck me, babe," Robin pleaded. "Fuck me while I fuck you."

And Micky did. She slid two fingers into Robin's wetness, and everything was washed away by a hurricane of lust raging through her flesh. Again.

CHAPTER TWENTY-NINE

The next Tuesday night, Micky drove Robin to her mother's house in Mosman. Not only because she'd had enough of her mother's relentless and, truth be told, very uncharacteristic phone calls asking if Micky had gone back to men yet. Gina was not usually caustic like that. Micky suspected that the reason she was acting out, was because, to her, Micky being in love with a woman was this big, new, unknown entity in her life. She needed to be able to put a face to the name. She needed to meet Robin. Moreover, Micky was proud to be able to introduce Robin as her partner. So it was with confidence more than with trepidation that she parked her car on the driveway of her mother's house.

"It's funny," Robin said before they got out of the car, "but this could so easily be a street in the suburb where I grew up."

Micky knew Robin well enough already to know that, even if she was nervous, she would never show it. She had prepped her the night before, telling her all about Gina, that she would be charm personified—no doubt about that—but her true feelings about Robin would reveal themselves during the lulls in conversation, those awkward pauses when she would take a second to breathe and relax. Micky would watch her mother like a hawk. But, in the end, as they walked to the back door, Micky wasn't too worried. She knew her mother and she knew Robin.

"Darling," Gina said as they walked into the door. She hugged Micky much more ferociously than she would on any other given day. Perhaps to postpone a little while longer the moment where she would shake hands with her daughter's lover and irreversibly make her acquaintance. Micky could speculate all she wanted, but she would never truly know what went on in her mother's head.

"And you must be Robin." Gina extended her hand.

"Very pleased to meet you, Mrs. Ferro," Robin said, sounding very official.

"Please, call me Gina." They shook hands, making this introduction seem more like the closing of a business deal.

Gina ushered them into the lounge and poured them coffee. She'd brought out the fancy china, which Micky took as a good sign. Then it dawned on Micky that, perhaps, Gina was as nervous about this as she and Robin were. After all, she'd only ever met one of Micky's significant others, and that was twenty years ago. While making this change in her life, Micky had asked her loved ones to change as well. Yet, the guilt she'd carried around for years, first for not being able to just take the leap and admit it, then for seeing another woman behind her family's back, had started to subside. The skin Micky found herself in these days fit her so much better, and no matter how awkward these first introductory conversations always were, Micky was a new and improved version of herself. Surely her mother could see that.

Besides, this was nothing compared to this coming weekend, when Olivia and Christopher would be home and Robin would come over for dinner.

"You're certainly very pretty," Gina said.

Micky had to giggle. Oh yes, her mother was very tense. But Micky was a mother herself, and even though she'd never been in a situation like this with one of her children—having to adjust to one aspect of your child's life being so different than you'd always believed—she felt for her mother. She wished they could skip to the second meeting, when the initial awkwardness would be out of the way, and they could truly learn how to behave around each other.

Micky could almost see how Robin was turning on the charm. She curled her lips into that bright, dazzling smile and said, "And I can certainly see where Micky gets her good looks from."

Gina was definitely a woman who prided herself on her looks, even more so as she progressed in age, but she wasn't that shallow that just someone telling her she looked good would win her over. At least, Micky hoped, it would set the tone for the rest of the conversation, and they could take it from there.

"Micky tells me you lived in Hong Kong and Singapore. I visited Hong Kong with my husband years ago. He'd always wanted to go. What a crazy, crazy place."

"It's madness," Robin replied, and just like that, they had found some common ground and the ice was broken.

"She's really nice," her mother said while Robin had excused herself to use the washroom. "So charming and well-spoken." She made a low humming noise in her throat. "Which reminds me of someone."

"Please don't say Darren. On the surface, there might be some similarities, but they're nothing alike, really."

"I can certainly see where they differ, dear. I have eyes in my head," Gina said smugly.

"Thanks for doing this, Mom. It means a lot to me."

"You don't need to thank me for meeting your new partner. I'm your mother. Of course it helps that my daughter's been smiling from ear to ear since she walked into my house." She put her hand over Micky's. "I'm happy for you. I really am."

Robin came back from the washroom, sat down at the table with them, and another, different kind of happiness washed over Micky. Perhaps she had Amber to thank for this as well, for leading by example and for showing Micky's mother that there's absolutely nothing wrong with being gay. Dear, dear Amber. Micky made a mental note to push her to go out with Martha already.

✴ ✴ ✴

Of all the people Micky had to introduce Robin to, her children were the ones she was most worried about. She was turning her from a mere notion into a woman of flesh and blood. Olivia and Christopher had only ever seen Micky with Darren, their father *and* a man. To become someone else, to be forever changed, in her children's eyes was the biggest challenge. By bringing Robin into their home, Micky wasn't only admitting to being a lesbian, she was also boldly stating that she was a human being with sexual interests, a thought that might not align itself well with being their mother.

Thankfully, after having a casual chat with Liv and Chris at The Pink Bean over muffins and juice, Sheryl had given Micky some *literature on sex-positive parenting*, which Micky had pored over but hadn't truly sunk in yet. What she'd taken away the most from the books Sheryl had pressed into her hands, was that Micky still had a lot left to learn herself.

Micky hadn't asked Amber to join her this time. They were *her* children, and she could do this alone. Yet, when the bell rang on Saturday evening to announce Robin's arrival, her heart leapt into her throat. Knowing very well who was standing outside their house waiting to be let in, Olivia didn't rush out of her seat and yell that she would get it. Micky hurried to the front door, and as it opened, the biggest ball of nerves uncoiled in her stomach. It wasn't so much that she automatically, magically, expected her children to like Robin just because she did, but just seeing her, having her near, gave her a confidence that had always been so foreign to her.

They hugged, and Micky inhaled Robin's familiar scent, bolstering her confidence even more.

"I just brought this." Robin held up a bottle of wine. "I had no idea what to bring for kids their age."

"No need. They're spoiled enough as it is."

"I thought I'd be less nervous after having met your mother this week, but I'm really tense. It feels like going on a job interview for a start-up run by people half my age. I feel like I need to be down with the kids, you know?"

"Relax. They're not monsters. I raised them, remember?"

"Off we go then." Robin squared her shoulders and walked into the living room.

Christopher jumped out of his seat. He'd insisted on wearing a pristinely ironed dress shirt, even though Micky had assured him that was by no means necessary, which had earned him more scorn from his sister. He offered Robin his hand, but Robin sidestepped him and pulled him into a hug.

Micky hadn't had a long conversation with Robin about this meeting the way she had before she'd taken Robin to meet her mother because some things simply needed to happen more organically. She'd told her about her children's characters, shown her treasured pictures from when they were younger, but she hadn't advised Robin on how to behave around them. Micky was sure Robin could figure that out herself.

Olivia had risen from the sofa as well and stood fidgeting uneasily with her hands. She wasn't wearing her usual teenage facade of indignation.

"Hi, Olivia." Robin pulled Liv into a hug as well, and Micky remembered how frightened she had always been of this moment. How the prospect of this was one of the biggest obstacles she'd had to overcome on this journey. And now there she stood. No matter how this evening played out, the most difficult part was already over. Robin was there in the house she shared with her children. They would eat a meal together—Micky had made macaroni and cheese because it was the kids' favorite—and chat and start their lives together as an out-of-the-ordinary family perhaps, but one that was a million times happier than the one Micky had broken up when she'd asked Darren for a divorce. Not that any amount of her personal happiness could ever undo that dreadful moment when she'd had to sit across from her children and tell them their mother and father didn't want to be together anymore. But this was life, and now they knew.

Micky could try to protect them all she wanted, could try to keep them stashed in a cocoon of fabricated, put-upon happiness and hope they wouldn't notice, but what service would that do them in the end?

They sat down at the table, and Chris made a display of pouring Robin and Micky a glass of red wine, and Olivia didn't even roll her eyes at him.

"When can I try some, Mom?" Chris asked, pointing at the wine.

"On your next birthday," Micky said, looking at her boy who was growing up so damn fast. "If you're lucky."

"Last time I asked, you said I could have a small glass on *your* next birthday, which is only a month away, Mom, so I might as well have some now. This is a special occasion, isn't it?"

Robin grinned. "You have excellent negotiating skills, Christopher."

"If he's having some, I'm having some," Liv butted in.

As the conversation carried on, Micky realized that this was all so much easier than she had always believed it would be. The biggest hurdle had always been the one in her head.

"Mom?" Liv said.

"Yes, honey."

"Can we have some wine or not?"

Micky shook her head. "No, darling, you can't. You're too young." They could try to play her all they wanted, Micky was still their mother, and she knew when to put her foot down.

CHAPTER THIRTY

"I used to come here at least twice a week," Micky said. She looked out over the ocean. It was her forty-fifth birthday, and Robin had taken the afternoon off to spend some alone time with her before the party tonight with her children, mother, and friends. Micky hadn't taken the morning off from serving coffee because it seemed like such an essential part of her by then. To wake up every weekday morning with a clear purpose: go to work. It wasn't the work itself, though Micky enjoyed that, too. She liked the customer interaction and picking up twenty-something lingo from Josephine and watching how Kristin stalked around the place, always with a sense of pride about her. She loved what the place had done for her, the confidence it had brought her and, more than anything, the woman it had introduced her to.

With Robin by her side, the ocean seemed a little bluer, the caps of the waves a little whiter. It was cold but sunny— the exact weather Micky would have ordered from the weather gods for her birthday if she could have.

"Remember when you took me to Bondi beach?" Robin leaned into her a little, warming Micky's flank. "You were so hot for me that day. You were basically squirming on your beach towel all afternoon."

"And you knew and loved it."

"Well, you know," Robin leaned her head on Micky's shoulder, "it's not every day I get to seduce a housewife from Mosman."

They both chuckled and inhaled greedily because the

air was always so different by the ocean. Micky had come there on her forty-fourth birthday as well, although then it was more out of lack of official celebration than anything else. She'd just signed the divorce papers a few months earlier and was still living in the house her children had grown up in. And, like every year, Micky had—foolishly— asked the ocean, "Where will I be one year from now?" This year, when the question flitted through her mind, not a trace of desperation, of desire for drastic change, clung to it. Micky had taken the leap. She had followed her best friend's advice, and there she stood, staring into the waves while all her dreams were coming true.

"I love you," Micky said, for the very first time to another woman in this context. It didn't feel as monumental as she had expected, perhaps because the entire year of leading up to her forty-fifth birthday had been one of firsts. Yet, the words made a warm glow erupt underneath her skin.

"I love you too, vixen." Robin had taken to calling her that in private as an inside joke. "And I have a birthday present for you." Robin turned to her. "I've known for a couple of days, but I waited to tell you until today. Next week, I'll be signing a new contract at work. One that keeps me here for at least two more years after this one's up."

Micky brought a hand to her mouth. She threw her arms around Robin and pulled her close while the crashing of the waves roared in her ears.

ACKNOWLEDGEMENTS

While writing this book I suffered, for the very first time, from something I hesitantly refer to as 'writer's block'. As a writer, when the words fail to come, it can be a big blow to your confidence. It's when my self-esteem is at its lowest that I rely on the beautiful, endlessly optimistic, kind person that is my wife the most. Without her, none of my books would ever have been written, but this one surely wouldn't have.

Special mention to my Sydney-based beta-reader Sarah, to my now regular beta-reader Carrie, and to new girl on the block, Laura. I greatly value your time and input.

Thank you also, Claire, for once again going on a typo-hunt for me.

I worked with my new editor Jason for the first time and his enthusiasm for the book, especially after I had such a hard time finishing it, bolstered my confidence… and his edits taught me a thing or two about grammar and spelling according to the Chicago Manual of Style, which is much appreciated.

I must also have the best and fastest Launch Team in the world, what with the way some of them read every new book in less than a day, and email me the sweetest comments. Your reviews and support help me and my books so much.

And, as always, endless gratitude to my Readers, for making each book a bigger success than the last. This journey I'm on is so rewarding and, frankly, bewildering, and none of it would be possible without you.

Thank you.

ABOUT THE AUTHOR

Harper Bliss is the author of the novels *The Road to You, Far from the World We Know, Seasons of Love,* and *At the Water's Edge,* the *High Rise* series, the *French Kissing* serial and several other lesbian erotica and romance titles. She is the co-founder of Ladylit Publishing, an independent press focusing on lesbian fiction. Harper lives on an outlying island in Hong Kong with her wife and, regrettably, zero pets. She enjoys talking about herself and her writing process (but mostly herself) on her weekly YouTube broadcast Bliss & Tell.

Harper loves hearing from readers and if you'd like to drop her a note you can do so via harperbliss@gmail.com

Website: www.harperbliss.com
Facebook: facebook.com/HarperBliss
YouTube: youtube.com/c/HarperBliss

Made in the USA
Lexington, KY
08 July 2018